CRISPUS HAD ALREADY PUSHED HIS WAY OUT THE door, and I shot off after him. I think I knocked over some girl's drink and stepped on somebody else's jacket, but I didn't hear their reactions. I did hear Norie, right behind me, saying, "Wait. I'm going with you."

I had to claw through a crowd of oglers at the door, who were pressing their faces against the glass and salivating to see a fight. By the time I got outside, Van and Crispus were already squaring off between two rows of cars. Their breath was hanging in the air between them like an atomic bomb cloud, but the explosion hadn't happened yet. They were still throwing foul language at each other, competing to see who could sound more like Satan himself. If I left out all the cuss words, there would barely be a sentence. As it was, they were interrupting each other so much I could only catch snatches.

Norie was cutting off the circulation in my arm. "Bri-*anna!*" she said.

I got my mouth close to her ear. "If this breaks loose, you get your white self out of here. They're not playin'."

"What are you doing?" Norie said.

I didn't answer. I wrenched away from her grip and yanked people aside by the sleeves of their flannels and jeans jackets as I headed for Crispus. The way I figured it, I had about ten more seconds to get between them and stop this, or it was going to bust open, and there would be no breaking it up without tear gas then.

Dear Parent,

Thank you for considering Nancy Rue's book for your teen. We are pleased to publish her Raise the Flag series and believe these books are different than most you will find for teens.

Tragically, some of the things our teens face today are not easy to discuss. Nancy has created stories and characters that depict real kids, facing real-life issues with real faith. Our desire is to help you equip your children to act in a God-pleasing way no matter what they face.

Nancy has beautifully woven scriptural truth and direction into the choices and actions of her characters. She has worked hard to depict the issues in a sensitive way. However, I would recommend that you scan the book to determine if the subject matter is appropriate for your teen.

Sincerely,

Dan Rich
Publisher

Raise the Flag Series BOOK 4

DO I HAVE TO PAINT YOU A PICTURE?

Nancy Rue

WATERBROOK
PRESS
COLORADO SPRINGS

DO I HAVE TO PAINT YOU A PICTURE?
PUBLISHED BY WATERBROOK PRESS
5446 North Academy Boulevard, Suite 200
Colorado Springs, Colorado 80918
A division of Bantam Doubleday Dell Publishing Group, Inc.

ISBN 1-57856-035-7

Published in association with the literary agency of
Alive Communications, Inc., 1465 Kelly Johnson Blvd.
Suite 320, Colorado Springs, Colorado 80920.

Printed in the United States of America
1998—First Edition

10 9 8 7 6 5 4 3 2 1

To Cheri Bladholm,
who shows the power art has when it comes
from the heart of God

"LOOK AT HER," NORIE VANDENBERGER SAID. "SHE'S grown to the stool."

I looked up from the canvas I was matting at Norie and the other four. The way their faces were all pokin' in the doorway, if I hadn't already been up to my scalp in paintings, girl, I'd have stopped right then and sketched them. Those girls were a living work of art.

Tobey L'Orange came over to the counter and stuck her chin right into my shoulder. "Did you forget?" she said.

"Forget what?"

Marissa Martinez was nodding. "She forgot."

"The Flagpole meeting!" That was Cheyenne Jackson, of course, our little freshman waif-child with a set of lungs like Tina Turner. She was tapping a finger on her fringe of dark bangs that hung down almost to her eyes. We're talkin' gigantic brown eyes. The only thing bigger on her face was her lips, which were gorgeous. I had to get around to painting them one day, but just then I had about all I could handle.

"I'm not going to lie to y'all," I said. "I forgot." I moved my gaze back to the canvas on the counter. "But even if I'd remembered, I couldn't have come. I have so much to do—"

"We know," Norie said. She stuck her stocky self on the stool next to me. "That's why we brought the meeting to you."

"You really think you're going to get this show up without *prayer?*" Cheyenne said.

"Listen to you, girl," I said. "Six months ago, if somebody had said, 'Cheyenne, you better pray to God,' you would have said, 'Who's God?'"

She happily wrinkled her nose and perched on the stool on the other side of me. Marissa and Shannon D'Angelo settled in across the counter from me and twisted their necks to look at the canvas upside down.

Anybody else would have made me turn it around. But to say those two weren't as aggressive as the rest of us was pretty much like saying Michael Jordan was tall. Now Marissa, she was Venezuelan and just a little bit shy. But Shannon was downright timid, and she couldn't have looked any more opposite from Marissa if they had been Night and Day themselves.

Marissa had café au lait skin, and shiny, straight, dark brown hair that was chopped off at her chin, the way no black girl could wear it even if she spent five hundred dollars in a beauty salon. But Shannon was so pale you could about see through her, and everything else about her was a shade lighter than it was on anybody else. Eyes just barely blue, like they were afraid to be too bright. Hair the color of sunlight just hangin' in the air. Clothes always pastel and flowy. The way I looked at it, I'd have to paint Marissa in oil, and Shannon definitely in watercolor.

Right now they stared politely at my *Voices of Violence,* and I knew they didn't have a clue what the thing was about, but neither of them would have said so if I'd threatened them with my matting knife. Now Cheyenne, on the other hand—

"So what's with all these mouths?" she said. She stuck her finger out to feel the painting, but Norie snatched it away.

"Don't touch it, child!" she said, tossing her boxy haircut and drilling her needle gaze into Cheyenne. "You don't go poking at a person's painting. It's art!"

"It's all right; it's dry," I said. "Barely."

Tobey was watching me real close like she does, with those soft brown eyes. Between them and the high, intelligent-looking forehead, girl, you would have sworn she was a psychiatrist.

"Are you stressing, Brianna?" she said.

"No," I said.

"Liar," Norie said.

Shannon giggled nervously.

"You could have fooled me," Cheyenne said. "You always look like you want to smack somebody when you get stressed out."

I tried not to smile as I looked up at her. "Mmm-mmm, truth from a babe's mouth."

"Well, who wouldn't be freaked out over something like this?" Tobey said. She raked a hand through her bubble of strawberry-blonde hair like she was the one stressing. "Your own art show in the library—everybody looking at your stuff—"

"If I ever get my 'stuff' in there," I said. At that point, if I'd had hair, I'd have been raking my hands through it. But I got tired of messing with it a while back and cut it as close to my head as I could. Everybody thought I was making some African statement or something. They just don't know what a black girl has to go through to take care of a head of hair.

Tobey nudged me. "What do you mean, if you ever get it in there?"

"I mean I have so many paintings to mat I can't even stop to eat lunch."

"No problem," Norie said. "I'll hook up an IV—"

"I can help mat," Marissa said. "I've done it before."

"I brought cookies," Shannon said. Then she shrugged as if she had just said something lame, which she had, but I did smile at her. I smiled at all of them.

Hard as I tried to keep a shell on myself—you know, kind of like on an M&M—I was having a harder and harder time hiding myself when I was around the Flagpole Girls. That was what we had started to call ourselves sometime in the fall. Seemed like we had to have a name after a while.

It started off just the six of us showing up for See You at the Pole day that morning in September. Thing is, God showed up, too. He must have, because we ended up meeting once a week during lunch to pray. I mean, right there in the theater lobby, girl, with people passing through, lookin' at us. And then something would come up for somebody—like Tobey having to accuse the track coach of something foul or Norie having to get herself out of a really bad situation with the Honor Society types or Cheyenne just about getting herself arrested—and we all started coming together.

And I'll tell you what, the kind of praying we did, we got some miracles to happen.

"Brianna," Norie said in her pointy voice. "Put that weapon down—"

"It's a matting knife."

"Well, give it a rest. Come on, you have time to gag down half a sandwich and pray for seven seconds."

I sagged on the stool, and I did put down the knife. "I'm going to need to pray a lot longer than that, girl," I said.

"You're going to get this all done, Brianna," Tobey said. "You've been working so hard."

"We said we'd help," Norie said. "Now, don't give me one of those little scalpels—all your paintings would be in ribbons—but I can at least keep Cheyenne from impaling herself on it or something."

"What's 'impaling' mean?" Cheyenne asked.

While Norie defined the word, I looked around my corner of the art room. There were only five more pieces to do before tomorrow. Marissa could probably do one—

"Okay," I said. "I'll let y'all help, if you do exactly what I tell you."

Shannon looked like she would rather take herself out with the matting knife than disobey me. Marissa was already nodding and halfway up. This kind of lump was in my throat, which I choked down before it could get any farther up. One thing about Brianna Estes, she did not cry.

"Just go on and measure for that one over there," I said to Marissa. "And Shannon, you double-check her. Then I'll come triple-check."

"Yikes," Tobey said, "if it has to be that exact, I ought to just go on a drink run for you."

"Get her something without caffeine," Norie said. "She's pumped up enough already."

"You get me a Dr Pepper, girl, or I won't make it through the afternoon," I said. I dug in my pocket, but Norie waved me off.

"We've got it," she said.

Of course they did. Norie's father was some kind of surgeon, and Tobey never seemed to be wanting for anything. But I still kept digging and pulled out two quarters.

"You take this money, girl," I said, "or I'm not drinkin' it."

"She won't either," Cheyenne said as she followed them out of the art room. "Ira says she won't go anywhere with him unless he promises to go Dutch—"

Her voice didn't fade out until she was all the way down the hall. I shook my head and went back to my canvas. Just beyond me, I could hear Marissa and Shannon talking real soft to each other the way they did.

Huh. Different as they were from each other, they couldn't have been any more different from me. Sure, we were all three Christians and all three committed to living the most Christlike lives we could. But girl, just being black meant I was walkin' a way different path from them. Those paths were as different, well, as black and white.

They might be helping me get this art show up, but some things about my life at King High they couldn't begin to understand. And I didn't even know the half of it right then, sitting there in that art room thinking my biggest problem was not embarrassing myself in that library the next day.

Huh. If only we had known. And if only, somehow, we could have stopped what was about to happen when the art show opened.

CHAPTER ONE

IT SHOULD HAVE BEEN ONE OF THE BEST DAYS IN MY whole eighteen-year-old life. But the minute Ira and I walked into the Jack-in-the-Box for the celebration, Dillon Wassen came up behind me and said, "You better start watchin' your back, you . . ."

Then, of course, he added the usual expletive people like him have to throw in when they're talking to people like me. Black people. African-Americans. People they think ought to be wiped off the face of the earth, and the sooner the better.

I wanted to turn around and chew him up one side and down the other so bad. Three things stopped me. One, I was pretty much walking on air, and I wasn't ready to come down yet. Two, the Flagpole Girls were about to show up. And three, my man, my Ira Quao, was with me.

"Ignore him," Ira whispered to me.

Dillon didn't hear him. Ira has this real low, soft voice you can barely hear when he *isn't* whispering. Plus, the Jack-in-the-Box was filling up fast with kids from King High who crowded in there at lunchtime. Dillon wasn't usually one of them. I'd heard him say one day to his shaved-headed buddies—loud enough so I'd hear him—that he wouldn't be caught dead eating at the same place where a bunch of . . . well, a bunch of People Like Me were touching the food.

"What do you want to eat, baby?" Ira said to me.

"Curly fries, for sure."

Dillon mouthed off something about those going straight to my . . . Let's just say, "fat behind" and let it go at that. You get my drift about the way this fool talked, I'm sure. I can't even quote him exactly because I'm not in the habit of spewing a bunch of mess out of my mouth.

Ira stared into my eyes with this real firm look and said, "Come on, baby, that isn't all you're going to have. What else?"

"Spicy chicken sandwich . . ."

"What?" Dillon said. "No chitlins?"

"And a Diet Coke—no, make that a regular Coke since we're celebrating."

Behind me, Dillon made one of those derisive hissing sounds guys like him are always making because they don't have the vocabulary of a chimpanzee.

"I thought you would want a watermelon for this occasion," he said.

I rolled my eyes at Ira. He just twitched his eyebrows at me.

"There she is," I heard somebody say from the doorway. I didn't even have to look to know it was Cheyenne.

"Let's party!" Tobey shouted from behind Cheyenne.

"Where's Marissa and Shannon and all them?" I said.

"They're riding over with Norie and Wyatt," Cheyenne said. "Me and Fletcher came with Tobey."

She was, of course, entwined at the fingers with Tobey's younger brother, Fletcher. They had this Romeo-and-Juliet thing going on—Fletcher the big-time preacher's son and Cheyenne the foster child from down on Seventh Street. The only thing missing was the feuding parents.

Cheyenne gave a big ol' grin and squeezed poor little Fletcher's hand.

"Cool paintings, Brianna," Fletcher said.

"Thanks," I said.

He high-fived me with his free hand. "I didn't understand them, but they're cool."

Dillon gave one of his hisses. "That's because you're not a—"

"So, what's everybody eating?" Tobey sang out. She was dazzling the whole place with her smile and doing the Tobey-thing, which was avoid confrontation for as long as she could. She didn't dazzle Dillon.

"They're havin' chitlins and fried chicken," he said. "And a side order of watermelon."

"Chitlins?" Cheyenne said, scowling up at the menu. "Are they new?"

Ira kept a stern hold on my arm, and I didn't say anything. But in spite of my art-show high, Dillon was getting right under my skin.

"There's Norie," Tobey said.

Norie pushed her way through the crowd with her man, Wyatt, right behind her. Wyatt came over and shook hands with Ira and sparkled his eyes at me from behind his glasses. Next to the word "conservative" in the dictionary you would find his picture, but he wasn't a geek.

"You are so talented," he said to me. "Today was the first time I ever saw any of your stuff. You're like the next Picasso or something."

"Go ahead on!" I said to him.

"Have you, like, studied some other painters?" he said. "Or is that your own style? I can't even draw stick people. This whole thing totally fascinates me."

I didn't have a chance to answer him. I felt something jab me in the back. I whirled around to see Dillon chewing on a plastic straw.

"Yeah," he said, "did you study any Ne-gro painters? Any scratchings on the monkey cage walls?" He turned to a kid in a black-hooded sweatshirt who was slouched behind him. "Ape art," he said to the kid.

The kid's mouth opened like a hole as he gave what I guess was supposed to be a laugh. I knew by the hollow sound of it that the kid was Garrick Byers. He had trouble speaking two words before he had to throw in some cussing.

"Yeah," Garrick said. "It looked like a baboon coulda done it."

Dillon gave me a close look. "A baboon did."

"There's your order, Ira," Norie said. She jerked her head toward the counter so her bangs flipped. I could tell she was ticked off, just like the rest of my group.

My African-American friends, on the other hand, were sitting ten feet away, holding our tables. You didn't see Harlan or James coming up to defend me, or Eden or Laraine. Especially not after the door opened, and Van stepped in. Then I think the French fries even stopped frying.

"Oh no," I heard Shannon whisper. Ira took a real tight hold on my arm, and out of the corner of my eye, I could see Wyatt putting his arm in front of Norie so she wouldn't go flying over there and get herself killed.

I'm only halfway exaggerating about that. Van Hessler was one of the meanest boys I ever saw, and coming from East Oakland like I did, I'd seen some nasty ones. I bet this boy looked hateful when he was *sleeping*.

"Maybe we should go somewhere else," Marissa whispered.

"Why?" Cheyenne said. She was still looking for chitlins on the menu.

Shannon gave her a poke and pointed at Van. Cheyenne scowled. "No way," she said. "We're not afraid of him." She looked quickly at me. "Are we?"

"Can I take your order?" the girl behind the counter said impatiently to Dillon.

He shook his head, and excitedly fingering his wannabe goatee, he plowed through two lines to reach Van, with Garrick on his tail. Any other time I'd have been poking Ira and asking how long he thought it would be before Garrick walked right out of those pants. But just then, I wasn't taking my eyes off those three.

They were standing in the doorway, their shaved heads bent together like three tulip bulbs. I wished they were. I'd gladly have buried all three of them in the dirt, head down, hoping something decent might sprout.

"We could go to Burger King," Shannon was saying.

Ira shook his head and picked up our tray. "It's going to be all right," he said. "We have some tables reserved over here."

He gave me the nod, the one that means, "You just stick by me, baby" and led the way to the tables where my brave black friends were practically cowering under their chairs. They were just behind the little half-wall that divides the "dining room" from the ordering area, right where we would be out of Van Hessler's sight.

We were almost there, when Mr. Mean himself cut into Ira's path. Tall and skinny, as if he had been stretched up by the top of his head, he looked at my man out of his ol' pot-clouded eyes and lifted his lip, like he smelled something bad.

"Excuse me," Ira said.

"There ain't no excuse forya," Van said.

Behind me, Dillon and Garrick laughed like Van had just run Jay Leno off his own show.

"Just let me by," Ira said.

"What did you say?" Van said. "What did you say to me?"

"Come on, man," Ira said wearily. "You're not going to keep us from eating here so give it up."

"Actually, that's not what we come for," Van said. "We come to talk to your woman about her 'art.'"

He said the word "art" as if he thought my work was like listening to somebody squeezing Styrofoam and then calling it "music." It was all I could do not to shove Ira aside, tray and all, and give that boy a piece of my mind.

"You got something for her, you say it to me," Ira said.

"That ain't the way I understood it works with you blacks," Van said. "I thought your women were the boss."

Ira didn't answer. Nobody did, but the whole place was listening. Ira put down the tray next to Eden. Her eyes were about popping out of her head, and she scrunched herself up next to Harlan, who looked as if he was about to throw up.

"So what's your problem?" Ira said to Van.

"My problem is that 'painting' she's got in the library."

"You went into the library?" I heard Norie say at my elbow. "I'm surprised you even knew where it was."

I reached out and squeezed my fingers around her wrist. This was no situation for her mouth.

"Which painting?" Ira said. "She has a whole show in there."

"Yeah," Van said. "Must be Colored Week."

"It's Black History Month," Ira said.

"That ain't history," Van said. "It's a bunch of lies."

"Art doesn't lie," I murmured.

"I'm talkin' about that one piece of trash," Van said. "That one with all the mouths."

"'The Voices of Violence,'" I said aloud.

He leveled his murky eyes at me, and his face looked even harder than before. "Yeah. How come all the mouths were white?" he said. "Why weren't there any big black fat lips like yours in there? You're the ones doin' all the screamin' 'bout your 'rights.'"

"If my people had their rights they wouldn't be screaming," Ira said.

"Then paint your own kind flappin'," Van said.

His long arm shot out, and his fingers hooked on to my lower lip. It was like they hung there for a whole, suspended moment before Ira chopped Van's arm with the side of his hand. Dillon and Garrick yanked me back.

Then a woman with an auburn braid got right in the middle of it all and said, "Stop this! Stop this now!"

EVERYBODY STOPPED BUT VAN. HE WAS STILL LUNG-
ing for Ira when the woman planted the heels of both hands
on his scrawny chest and said again, "You *stop* it!"

Ira was all over me, glaring at Dillon and Garrick, who
didn't show any signs of going to the aid of their leader. By
then everybody, including Van, had realized the woman with
the red hair was Ms. Race, our principal's secretary.

What they didn't know was that she was the Flagpole
Girls' mentor. When she was around, we started to feel our
Cheerios. Although Marissa and Shannon were still frozen to
the floor, Norie took a step forward with Tobey right behind
her. Cheyenne squeezed her little sweet self in there, too, but
I grabbed her by the arm.

"I strongly suggest you leave," Ms. Race said to Van.

"This ain't school property," Van said, lip still turned up
like he had done it with a curling iron.

"You attack these students and it's school business," she
said.

Van hissed, and Dillon and Garrick echoed him. Shifting
his eyes back to Ira and holding them there, Van jerked his
head toward the table Laraine, Eden, James, and Harlan had
just vacated. James and Harlan were heading out the door,
and I could already see Laraine's cornrows and Eden's sleek
bob moving toward Harlan's beat-up Buick. Those were some
brave folks.

As Ms. Race watched, Van sat down on his tailbone at the table, and the other two flanked him like a pair of skinhead bookends. Ms. Race gave them one last long look before she moved back toward the line.

"I've never eaten here before," she said to me. "What's good?"

I grinned at her. That was one strong woman.

Our forty-six-minute lunch period was almost half over by the time everybody ordered and we crammed into two tables in the back corner. Ms. Race said she would write us all passes to get into class late. Her face was dead serious when she said, "I think this is a little more important right now."

"I sure wish Diesel had been here," Cheyenne said.

"How come he isn't?" Tobey said.

"He was in the middle of changing a carburetor or something. You can't just leave your pan dripping. That's what he said when we went by the auto shop. That's how come me and Fletcher rode with Tobey—not that I don't like riding with you, Tobe—but when your heater's not working, that car gets cold!"

"Get to the point, girl," I said dryly. Mmm-mmm, that girl could run off at the mouth.

"Anyways, if Diesel had been here, he would have kicked some tail."

That probably was true. Cheyenne's foster brother was way over six foot and had arms the size of most guys' thighs.

But Ms. Race was shaking her head. "I'm not interested in seeing any tail-kicking," she said. "No violence for any reason."

"I agree," Wyatt said.

Norie paused over her taco. "That's very idealistic and all that, but what if old Skinhead Van starts swinging a chain or something. What are we supposed to do, just stand there?"

"'We' don't need to do anything," Ms. Race said, "except run for the nearest adult." Her gray eyes seared the table. "I mean it, gang. This is serious stuff, and I don't want any of you trying to handle it on your own."

Norie put down her taco, and I could almost hear Tobey groaning. Norie, co-editor of the school newspaper, was getting all juiced up for a good argument. This was going to show up in an article, sure as I was sitting there. I could see it in that little needle gaze she was forming.

"Okay, so say Van or one of his little cronies corners Brianna in the hall, and by some miracle she gets away from him and comes to you. What are you going to do?"

"Take it straight to Mr. Holden," Ms. Race said. "Call security and have them haul the kid in. 'Van,' that's his name?"

"Yeah," Norie said. "And then what?"

"Mr. Holden will hear both sides of the story, and then the proper disciplinary action is taken. End of story."

I put down my own sandwich. A funny taste was forming in my mouth. "So you're saying I'd confront this dude in some vice principal's office?" I said.

"I think that's how it works."

"Uh-huh," I said. "And then I get called every vile name that's ever been thought up every time I walk down the hall. I get people spittin' on me in the locker room. I get—"

"Then you turn them in again," Ms. Race said.

"Mmm-mmm," I said. I sat back and folded my arms.

Ms. Race lost interest in her lunch, too. Matter of fact, just about everybody had quit eating by then.

"I don't always agree with the system at school," Ms. Race said. "But at times like this, it's all we have. You're protected there, Brianna. You're not when you're out here—not really."

I didn't answer. Neither did Ira. It got real weird at the table.

Remarkably, it was Shannon who spoke up first. "I knew some kids had been mean to you, Brianna," she said. "But I didn't know it was this big of a problem."

"Of course you didn't," I said, more sharply than I meant

to. "You walk around looking like some kind of porcelain doll, who's gonna give you any grief?"

"I'm sorry," she said. She slunk behind her soda. "I didn't know."

"How bad are those guys, really?" Tobey said.

We weren't *too* obvious at that point, all of us glancing over our shoulders at the skinhead table. Van and his boys didn't miss it. Every one of them slit his eyes at us like we were a bunch of snakes that needed getting rid of. Our group's heads snapped back so fast it would have been comical if I hadn't been getting my back up.

"They're badder than anything you've come up against," I said.

"Bad as East Oakland?" Norie said.

"No way," Fletcher said.

Tobey gave him a poke. "How would you know?"

"I watch TV!"

I shook my head at Norie. "The two short ones are wannabes. I'm not saying they wouldn't break out a knife or something, but neither of them has ever really used one, I bet. But Van, he's a whole other thing."

"So let's not give them any reason to," Ms. Race said. "We're not Sutro."

I grunted. Sutro was the Reno high school that was smack in the middle of a mostly African-American and Latino neighborhood. They had it all over there. I knew because I'd gone there for a semester my freshman year when Mama and I first moved from Oakland. After we got to know Ira and his parents at church, Ira's father helped me get a variance to go to King, even though we were zoned for Sutro. He explained that I was a talented artist, and I needed to be able to take advantage of the great art program at King. But it was more so I could get away from all that mess they were into over there. It was nothin' to be standing at your locker and have somebody come up and try to make a drug sale. If Sutro didn't have a stabbing or a gun wasn't found in somebody's

car every week, they about declared a school holiday to celebrate.

"The black kids over there think they have to fight their
battles on their own," Ms. Race was saying. "Now there's a
group of them that's every bit as bad as the white supremacists who are after them."

"Brothers of X," Norie said. "The *Gazette-Journal* had an
article on them." I could see her writing one of her own in her
head. She about never quit thinking like a newspaper editor,
she and Wyatt, who was the other editor for the school paper.
They were a pair.

"Like Generation X?" Marissa said.

"No," Wyatt told her. "Malcolm X."

"Who's Malcolm X?" Cheyenne said.

While Wyatt leaned in and gave her a crash course
in black history, I looked at Ms. Race. "I don't think we need
to worry about the African-Americans at King turning into
the Brothers of X," I said. "Or didn't you notice how they
beat it out of here like they had the devil himself chasing
them?"

Shannon shuddered. "They *did* have the devil chasing
them."

"You're probably right," Ms. Race said. "But I doubt those
kids at Sutro planned to turn into what they've become. It just
happened because they tried to fight violence with violence.
It doesn't work."

Next to me, Ira cleared his throat. All that time, he barely
had made a sound, but I could tell he was about to come out
with something worth listening to. That was the way my man
was. He didn't believe in saying anything unless he had something to say. Then everybody better listen, because he was
only goin' to say it once.

"Dudes like Van have a hate that goes deeper than some
vice principal can get at," Ira said. "That's why the Brothers of
X started. You can't fight that kind of hatred with a referral to
the office and an in-school suspension."

Ms. Race folded her hands. "Still, the real answer is equality."

"Uh, I don't think we're going to get equality by sending them to detention," Norie said.

"How are we going to get it?" Cheyenne said. "Do we need a Plan of Action?"

Bless little Cheyenne's heart. She thought the Flagpole Girls could wipe out three hundred years of evil thinking with one of our little campaigns.

"So you're saying we can't really *change* anything," I said to Ms. Race. "You're saying we just have to go by the rules and hope they work to keep us from getting our throats slit."

Shannon looked like hers had already been slit. Marissa didn't look much better.

"I think that's what we should do while we're taking peaceful measures to gain true equality in our society," Ms. Race said. She smiled, crinkling the freckles on her nose. "I sound like some kind of brochure, don't I?"

"Throw in a few more we-all-must-be-one phrases," Norie said. "Then you'll have it."

"This isn't a joke, people!" I said.

I felt Ira's hand on my knee. There was an urgency in it that shut me right up.

"We ought to pray, guys," Tobey said.

Everybody nodded and groped for each other's hands. I couldn't help glancing over my shoulder at the skinheads, but they were gone.

Tobey started us off, and then the others spoke up. Their voices were like Ben-Gay on my muscles—until Ms. Race prayed.

"We already think of Brianna and Ira as being just like us," she said to God. "Please open the eyes of the rest of our world to that same fact. We are all the same in your sight."

Something about that got me in the throat. I could feel myself jerking my neck the way I do when I'm about to snap somebody's head off with my next words. And I wasn't even sure why.

"Be with the skin—with Van and Dillon and that other guy," Norie said, tightly. "Much as I hate to say it."

"And Lord," I said in a burst that was more air than words, "give me the strength to deal with this the way You want me to."

When our heads came up, I could feel Ms. Race looking at me. I looked right back at her.

"Somebody once said to be careful what you pray for," she said. "Because you might get it."

"What's wrong with that?" Cheyenne said. She looked at Fletcher as if she expected him to answer.

"Sounds good to me," he said.

Norie was intrigued. "You pray for a Caribbean cruise; you get it—what's the problem?"

Ms. Race grinned. "But it might not be on the Princess Line," she said. "You could end up hauling Haitian refugees through a hurricane."

"You make God sound like some kind of twisted practical joker," Tobey protested.

"No," Ms. Race said, "I'm just pointing out that prayers are answered a lot of times through the circumstances of our lives."

"Huh?" Cheyenne said.

I was having a hard time with that one myself.

"Okay," Ms. Race said. "You ask for a loving heart, but suddenly you're overwhelmed with people who are hard to love. You ask for a hospitable spirit, and you can pretty much expect people to start showing up at your door when you've got PMS."

"I hate that," Wyatt said.

"So what are you saying?" I said. "I asked for strength."

"I'm just saying be ready. God's going to give you opportunities to build your spirit-muscles." She looked at me with her eyes all soft. "I'd have asked for protection, myself."

I didn't say anything. None of us spoke as we picked up our trash and went for the door. But I was sure thinking stuff. *You would have asked for protection? Well, you're not me, are you, Ms. Race? You don't know anything about my life!*

I stopped at the tray drop-off and considered that for a second. Interesting. On the way *to* the table I'd been thinking how strong she was. But she didn't want *me* to be strong.

"You okay, Brianna?" she said behind me.

I jerked my neck. "I'm fine," I said. "But thanks for asking."

"Come to my office to get passes before you go to class," she called to all of us as we scattered to our cars. "But don't dilly-dally."

She took off in her car, an orange thing she called "Señora," and Tobey and Norie followed in "Lazarus" and "Iggy" respectively. But when Ira and I got in his truck, he just sat there behind the wheel. I stuck my hands in my armpits and shivered.

"Start this thing up, honey," I said. "I'm about to freeze my tail off."

"I'm not," he said. "I'm hot."

I gave him a hard look. He was biting at his lip and clutching the steering wheel like he was keeping it from flying off.

"What?" I said.

"I'm waiting for them to leave," he said.

"They left."

"No, them."

He darted his eyes toward the corner of the parking lot and then planted them back on the wheel. I glanced over and caught Van Hessler glaring at us from behind the windshield of his black Cherokee. Mama had once commented to me that some of the kids at King High had better cars than she ever hoped to own. Funny, I'd never thought of Van Hessler coming from a rich family. I'd always thought of him as pure white trash.

"What are they going to do, follow us back to school?" I said.

"It's not the following I'm worried about," Ira said.

I scooted farther from him so I could look square at his face. "You really think they're going to try to run us off the road in broad daylight?"

"I don't know," Ira said. "But it isn't over."

"You didn't buy into what Ms. Race said either, did you?"

"No. I don't think she knows what she's talking about."

It was funny. At the time she was saying that stuff, I didn't either. But something about the way Ira was talking made my curly fries turn on me.

"Maybe not," I said. "But what else are we going to do?" I squeezed his leg. "You're always telling me to calm down and back off, and I do it."

"That's right," he said.

"So?"

His eyes went to the corner of the parking lot and followed the Cherokee to the driveway. He reached down and turned the key.

"Ira," I said, "what are you thinking?"

"Nothing," he said.

His voice was as soft as always, his eyes as calm. But his silence was running up my backbone like a fingernail up a chalkboard.

"Ira, *what?*" I said. "You're thinking something. Now you tell me what it is."

"I'm just thinking about how to keep you out of trouble," he said.

We pulled out into the intersection of McCarran Boulevard and MaeAnne, and I stared at him. "What are you talking about?"

"We never had that much trouble with the skinheads before," he said. "They glared at us, we glared back. No big deal, right?"

"Unless you count them hissing at me in the halls and whispering rude things about my body parts," I said.

"Now since you did that painting, that's only going to get worse."

"You're saying I did that painting on purpose to get them all riled up?"

"You didn't do it on purpose, but it sure did the job now, didn't it?" He smiled at me, but I definitely did not smile back. I knew my face was "turning into a piece of charcoal," as my mother always said when I was about to pitch a fit.

"Now don't get all huffy," Ira said. "I'm going to take care of this."

"What—what is it you think you have to take care of, Ira Quao? You going to apologize for my art?"

"No, baby."

"Then what?"

"It's a guy thing."

We were at the corner of MaeAnne and King Drive waiting for the light to change. I almost had my hand on the door handle. "I can't believe you said that. You take that back, boy, or I am out of this car!"

"I didn't mean it that way, not like it's a thing a girl can't handle—"

"Uh-*huh*."

"I meant it isn't the way *you* would handle it."

"Oh," I said. I crossed my arms across my chest as we headed up the last street toward the school. "You mean, the way the doctor's son would handle it, not the way the sister on the poverty line would handle it."

"Baby, come on, you know that isn't what I meant."

"Then what are you going to do, Ira? We're either in this thing together, or we're not."

He put the truck in neutral in a parking place at the edge of the lot, turned off the key, and shut down the heater, all in this neat, meticulous way that was about to drive me nuts. I grabbed his hands and held them hard and made him look at me. His brown eyes were like a luscious pair of caramels, his head was close cropped and perfect shaped, and his lips pursed together all wiselike. But I didn't care how drop-dead gorgeous he was at that moment. I just wanted the truth, and he wasn't about to give it to me.

"You have five seconds to tell me what you're thinking, or I'm gone," I said. "We're not going to do it like this."

"Yes, we are," he said.

"You're not going to tell me."

He shook his head.

I gave him one last chance. I held on to his hands like I was keeping him from dropping off a cliff, and I drilled my eyes into his. He didn't even blink.

"All right then," I said. I yanked myself away and fumbled for the lock.

"I'll see you after school," he said.

"No," I said, "you won't. I'll find my own way home. Thank you very much."

I slammed the door and left him sitting there, staring at the steering wheel.

CHAPTER THREE

PEOPLE KEPT COMING UP TO ME THE REST OF THE day saying things like, "Awesome art, Brianna!" and "Who knew you could paint like that? Man!" But the kick had been taken out of it. Even after I took the city bus home, and Mama came in and asked me what the show was like and what people said, I couldn't work up any real excitement.

"What is wrong with you, girl-child?" she said. She put her hands on her hips as she stood in the opening between our dinky living room and the even dinkier kitchen-eating area. Sitting on the thrift-store couch, I shrugged.

"Don't give me that," she said. She came toward me like a cat, head down, ears all back, like she was about to pounce. I had to laugh at her.

"I'm not playing with you," she said. She sank into the beanbag that faced the couch and folded up her long legs. "I thought you'd be dancin' over this thing. Now, come on, what's up?" Before I had a chance to answer, this guilt-stricken look crossed her face. "Is this because I didn't come in today? Now, baby, I told you I took Thursday afternoon off so I could come in, but it just wasn't going to happen today, not with payroll to get out—"

"It isn't that, Mama," I said. "I know you have to work."

"All right then, you best start talking." She crossed her arms just the way I do and waited.

I waited, too. The question wasn't whether I was going to

tell her about Ira. Mama and I were more like sisters than mother and daughter after all we had been through together. It was just a question of how much of the stuff leading up to it I was going to say. We hadn't had to face anything like this since Oakland. I didn't know how much she could handle again.

"So do I have to get me a switch, girl-child?" she said.

"Like you would really whip me," I said.

"Don't you think I won't, coming in here looking like you do. If I don't get something out of you soon, I might consider it."

I watched her smile at me. I'd spent a lot of time studying my mama's face. She was the best subject for a painting, but I hadn't tried to do one of her alone. I think I was afraid I couldn't capture what she had on canvas. She looked softer, rounder, more feminine than I did. People always told me I was beautiful—I guess it was true—but it was in a more stark, intense way than Allegra Estes's beauty. Her looks were warm. Earthy.

'Course, they had been hardened by a difficult life. She was only thirty-seven, but she had puffy places under her eyes and lines around her mouth. The thing I wasn't sure I could get to come out in paints was that she had the character of somebody who's overcome more than most people ever see, and that kind of beauty goes beyond handsomeness.

She was getting prettier all the time, I thought. She had looked tight to me when I was growing up, but those were the hard years. Now that she had decided to pull her life together, she seemed to be falling back on a cushion of happiness she had known when she was a little girl. The kind of happiness I hadn't known until I was about fifteen years old.

Now she wore her hair down to her shoulders, immaculately groomed into loose curls. Her skin was paler than mine. She had a café mocha look going on, where I was like the color of a coffee bean with my hair cut as close to my head as

I could get it. I was not going to pay sixty dollars every six weeks to sit in some beauty shop and have some ol' hot combs sizzling against my oiled scalp just so I could be a commercial, mahogany princess with glossy black curls.

Anyway, she had smaller eyes than mine, and they were shiny black. Mine were big and serious. But what distinguished her from me most, what made her look young again, was her sweet smile. She didn't flash it around like a beauty contestant, but when Mama did decide to smile, she just went on and did it. She wasn't cautious about it like me. It just dawned across her face and lit up her eyes. Her smile made you think of sunshine and giggling in bed with your sisters and brothers and choosing an ice cream flavor.

She stopped smiling at me now.

"Something's really eating at you," she said. "Why don't you come on and tell me what it is?"

I studied my nails. "I had a fight with Ira."

"On the day of your opening?" she said. "That boy better have had a real good reason!"

"How do you know it wasn't me that started it?"

She laughed. "You probably did. What happened?"

I picked my words carefully. "We went out to celebrate, the Flagpole Girls and some of the guys, you know . . ."

"Uh-huh."

"And these white guys started dissing my paintings."

"What white guys?"

She didn't miss a trick. She was already sitting straight up on the beanbag, eyes narrowing.

"Just some fools," I said. "You know, the kind that's always hissing at me in the halls."

"Go on."

"So we got into a discussion about it at the table, about whether to come back at them or what."

"I want to hear what 'or what' is," Mama said.

"Ms. Race said we ought to turn them in at school if they harassed us. She said not to get ourselves involved in it."

Mama was watching me intently.

"I don't think it would do much good, personally," I said.

"And Ira did," Mama said. "Which only makes sense. Now, baby, he's lived a different life than you have. He's had money on his side."

I shook my head. "He didn't buy it either. But he got it in his head that he's going to 'take care of me.' No, what did he say? Oh, 'keep me out of trouble.'"

"If he figures out how to do that, you tell him to tell me. I've been trying to figure that out for eighteen years!"

I frowned across our footlocker-covered-with-a-scarf coffee table. "He wasn't playing though. He has something in his mind, but he wouldn't tell me."

"Something? Like bad something?"

"Like 'I'll take care of this, baby. Don't you worry none about it.' I hate that."

She unfolded herself from the beanbag and came over to sit beside me. Her hand was cool and smooth on my arm. "Ira is not a stupid boy," she said. "Whatever it is he has in mind, I don't think you need to worry about it."

"That isn't the point!" I said.

"The point is, he wouldn't tell you."

I shrugged. "Maybe."

"That's exactly it, and you know it. You always have to know every detail, or you work yourself up into a charcoal-hissy."

"Well, it's about me! I think I have the right to know. I don't have that many friends my own race. We at least ought to trust each other."

"Which is exactly why you shouldn't let this go on," Mama said. She ran her hand down the back of my head. She always said she liked the feel of it, all woolly and natural.

"You think so?" I said.

"I've told you before, the only bad thing about leaving Oakland was coming to a place where there are so few blacks. Unless you want to count those troublemakers in the Sutro neighborhood, except for those families at the church, baby, we are alone here. We have to work at those relationships."

I crossed my ankles on the footlocker. "If he calls me, I'll try to work it out with him."

She sniffed. "If he calls you. Listen to you."

"What?"

"If you really want to work this out, you call him."

Before I could turn on her, she raised both hands, palms to me, and shook her head. "I'm just saying what I would do."

"You would crawl back?"

"This isn't crawlin', girl-child! Mmm-mmm, Miz Thang, you got some pride on you!"

I couldn't help grinning as she grabbed me gently around the neck and pulled me close to her.

"There's enough hatin' going on," she said to me. "Let's not make more by being stubborn."

I nodded. "I'll call him."

"I'll start dinner. I bought us something special to celebrate your show."

I went to the kitchen and picked up the phone on the wall while she pulled two stuffed Cornish game hens out of the refrigerator. I put my hand over the mouthpiece as the phone rang on the other end.

"Mama, we can't afford those!" I said.

"You hush up, girl," she said. "We're celebrating. Besides, you're eating Campbell's soup the rest of the week."

"Hello?" said a smooth, female voice.

I felt a flutter of relief. It wasn't Ira's mother answering but his older sister, Koretta.

"Hey, Korie," I said. "Let me talk to Ira, would you?"

There was an unnatural pause. "He's not home yet," she said. "We thought he was with you."

I grunted. "No. We had a little difference of opinion. I took the bus home."

"So, you want me to smack him when he gets home, or just have him call you?"

"Both," I said.

I could hear somebody else talking in the background.

"It's Brianna," Koretta told whoever it was.

There was another weird silence. I knew it must be Ira's mother.

"Thanks," I said. "Talk to you later."

"Let's go shopping when I'm on spring break," she said. "You're off, too. That's only two weeks away."

"Sure," I said. "'Bye."

I hung up the phone and grunted again.

"What's wrong?" Mama said.

"Koretta wants to go shopping with me."

"What did you tell her?"

"Did you hear me say, 'Sure, TJMaxx or Sak's Fifth Avenue?'"

Mama shook her head at me and shooed me out of the kitchen.

"Don't you need help?" I said.

"No, this is your night. I have it handled."

She pushed me into the beanbag and picked out a record to put on our ancient turntable. We were about the only people I knew, except maybe at Cheyenne's house, who still played records—records we picked up at yard sales or checked out from the library. Mama selected a Coltrane from her stack of jazz albums and adjusted the volume. I started to talk before she even settled herself on the big floor cushions beside me and the saxophone started to wail.

"I know," I said. "This isn't about being rich. It's about having a life we can be proud of."

"That's right. TJMaxx might come into it later, but for now, we have everything we need."

Looking around at our living room, I thought how some people might find that hard to believe. In addition to the twenty-five-dollar couch and the "creative" chairs and coffee table, we had the record player on a planks-and-bricks bookcase with scarves in the liberation colors of red, gold, and green hanging from it. And there was the table from the Salvation Army that you had to put a matchbook under the one leg to keep it from wobbling. The walls were covered with my paintings, all of them abstracts except for the one of Mama and Prentice taken from a photograph when he was two.

"I know, Mama," I said. "We have it all."

"You need me to go through it with you again?"

"I don't know. Maybe."

She took that as a yes. "I have a decent job over there at the school district. At least we have benefits. We have us some nice friends, both of us. And Lord knows the church is the best of it. That's worth everything."

I nodded.

"No more break dancing in the street and rapping on the corner and hanging out at house parties 'cause that's all there is to do," she said.

I nodded again.

"That the good Lord has taken me in after I turned my back on him twenty years ago. Honey, I'd live on the street just to have that." She tossed her hair back and laughed. "This place isn't much, but it's the Taj Mahal next to what we came from, and we have three thrift stores within walking distance."

"Walking *to* them isn't so bad," I said. "It's dragging the furniture home I have a problem with!"

"A couch just won't fit in the backseat of an Escort. Period."

"Yeah, but you can't say I didn't try."

"Nobody can say we don't try, that's for sure. That's how we know we are somebody."

Yeah, we had that part down to a science. We were constantly reminding ourselves who we were. That was why we saved up to go out to dinner once a week—we're talking Denny's or McDonald's, now, but it was something. That was why we each wore something new every week, even if it was a new color of nail polish. That was why we always had music going, why we went to church. Mama told me at least once a week, "We can't wait till disaster hits to connect with God; we know that now. We have to stay connected to Him and ourselves all the time."

She grinned at me now and went over to turn up John Coltrane. "You just lay back and listen to some good music," she said. "I'm going to work on our dinner."

Mama had a way of making it all right. She hadn't always taken the time to do that for me, which was probably why I appreciated it so much now.

The first ten years of my life I hardly ever saw her because she was working two and three jobs just to pay the rent on that hole of an apartment in the projects. I saw more of Prentice than she did. Even though he had only been four years younger, I'd about raised him. Fed him his meals, got him off to school, put him into bed before she came home all worn out and snappy. I don't think she ever yelled at him. I took his share.

I lost a lot growing up the way I had. We all lost a lot that evening at the park.

But we had gained some, too. After four years of hating, Mama said we just couldn't live like that anymore. After wondering since the day she had left *her* Mommy's house how there could possibly be a God, she had gone back to the Lord, and then she'd brought me to Him. She started to forbid me to go to street parties and got me drawing—from comic books, on the walls in our apartment, anything to turn me around. When it was clear we were in the lap of Satan in East Oakland, we'd come here—

The phone jangled me out of my thoughts.

"Baby, could you get that?" Mama called out. "I have my hands in the dishwater."

"If this place had a dishwasher, you wouldn't have that problem," I said.

I caught her grinning when I got to the kitchen.

"Bite your tongue right off," she said. "We have hot water, don't we?"

I answered the phone on its second ring.

"Hello?" I said, still grinning.

"Brianna, it's me."

"Who?" I said. I didn't recognize the voice. All I could hear was the crying.

"Koretta," she said.

My smile faded. "What's wrong?"

"It's Ira."

Suddenly it didn't matter that we weren't in East Oakland in the projects eating cold beans in the dark. The phone call sounded the same. *It's your daddy. It's Prentice. It's Ira.*

"No," I said.

"He's been in an accident. They have him at St. Mary's."

"No."

"It's bad. You better come on down here."

"No," I said one more time.

But as I hung up the phone, I knew it was all too real.

Again.

CHAPTER FOUR

I DIDN'T SAY A WORD ALL THE WAY TO THE HOSPITAL. Mama never stopped talking.

"Now you know Dr. Quao knows what he's doing. He'll make sure Ira gets the best—now you *know* that. Besides, I'd stake my life on Koretta's blowing this out of proportion. She gets hysterical over every little thing. You remember when her mother had her gall bladder out? You would have thought the woman was at death's door . . ."

I was glad it took only five minutes to drive from our place to St. Mary's. I knew she was only trying to help, but I was about to tell my own sweet mama to please shut up.

Koretta stood up when we walked into the ER. Her face was all swollen from crying. Mama was right about that part. The girl threw her arms around me—24-karat gold bracelets and all—and sobbed into my neck.

"Is he dead?" I whispered to her.

She shook her head and kept crying. Over her shoulder I looked at Ira's mother. She stretched her long, perfectly manicured fingers across her mouth and closed her eyes. Mama went and sat next to her. I got myself away from Koretta and went right over there.

"What happened?" I said. "What . . . how is he?"

Mrs. Quao pulled into herself like a snail.

"You all right, Winnie?" Mama said to her.

Ira's mother smoothed the long fingers over her shiny

workout pants. "I won't be until I know Ira's going to come out of this."

"What do you mean, 'come out of it'?" I said.

"It was a head-on collision," she said, looking at me "head-on." "Both his legs are broken. They think he has a neck fracture. Heaven knows what else."

I went cold. "Could he die?" I said.

She cut through me with a look.

"We've been here before, Winnie," Mama said, rubbing Mrs. Quao's sleeve. "We don't know how to dance around questions like that."

She shook her head. "There could be permanent damage. We'll know after surgery."

"Surgery!" I said.

"Yes, surgery." Mrs. Quao leveled her eyes at me. "You should have thought about that a long time ago."

I had no idea what she was talking about, but I could feel my own eyes hardening. Mrs. Quao had never been that crazy about me, but something was up with the woman. Mama's fingers folded around my arm and pulled me down to the chair on the other side of her.

"She's just in shock," she whispered to me.

"Daddy!" Koretta screamed.

I was sure people under anesthetic in the O.R. stirred. She flung herself into the arms of a tallish man with graying hair, Dr. Quao.

"It's all right," Ira's father said. "He's come to."

Mrs. Quao sprang from her seat, but Dr. Quao took hold of her by both arms and looked over her sleek-haired head at me.

"He's asking for you, Brianna," he said.

"No, now I am *not* going to stand for that!" Mrs. Quao said.

He looked down at her and murmured something. She flounced herself back to the seat and wouldn't even look at

Mama. Koretta ran to her mother, and they carried on together. I got right in Dr. Quao's face.

"He wants to see me?" I said.

He nodded, took my arm, and steered me back through the emergency room.

I'd loved Ira's father from the first time I'd met him, even before I had started going out with Ira. That didn't happen to me with many people. I tended to be from the guilty-until-proven-innocent school of thought. But he was so gentle. Everything about him was gentle, from the boylike way he pronounced proper English in his Ghanaian accent to the way he closed his eyes and nodded and smiled when you were explaining something to him, like he was really listening. I loved him, but never more than I did right then. As we moved past the counters, curtained cubicles, and parked gurneys, he was talking softly close to my ear, telling me everything.

"They have to perform surgery for the fractures in his legs and neck," he said. "He appears to have no internal injuries, however. He will live, Brianna. Don't worry; he will live."

"Will he be the same?" I said.

He smiled. "Now are we sure we want that?"

I gave him a smile back, but I knew it was trembly. I was shivering like I was freezing to death.

He stopped me outside a set of curtains. "Wait here. I'll come out for you."

I didn't trust myself to answer him. My teeth were chattering so hard I had to clamp down on them to keep my face still. Arms wrapped around my body, I stood there and shook.

It was all too familiar. The antiseptic smell. The straight-faced, hurrying people in nondescript green and white and blue. The sound of the curtains being swept closed.

The curtain next to me set up a breeze as it slid open. Two guys in short green tops hauled out a gurney, and I looked up. My shaking stopped. So did everything else.

A shaved head stuck out from under the covers, eyes closed, mouth slack above its scraggly goatee. I'd never seen Dillon Wassen unconscious before, but I knew it was him. I'd been right about the skinheads. They did look cruel even when they were sleeping.

As they rolled him away, my heart started to beat again, and the shaking took up at double speed. There was only one way Dillon could have ended up in the emergency room at the same time as Ira. Either that, or this was the biggest co-incidence in history.

"Brianna?" Dr. Quao whispered to me.

I whipped around and followed him behind the curtain. At that point, I forgot Dillon Wassen. All I could think about was my baby, strapped down on a table with bottles draining into both arms and his eyes searching the ceiling for something to hold on to.

"He cannot be moved," Dr. Quao cautioned me.

I nodded and got as close to the table as I could without climbing up on it. It was hard to get to where I could look into Ira's swollen eyes so he didn't have to turn his head. The minute I did, they started filling.

"Hey," he whispered.

"Hush up," I said. "If you talk, you'll move."

He closed his eyes and tried to smile, but his face puckered up. Tears slithered down his cheeks in little wet trails.

"Does it hurt real bad, honey?" I said.

"I'm just scared."

"Your daddy says it's going to be all right."

"No," he said.

"Yes!"

"No, I'm scared about you."

I shook my head. "I'm not mad at you anymore, honey. Just forget about that. I love you."

He ran his tongue across his lips and caught some tears. "Daddy?" he said.

I turned to look. Dr. Quao had disappeared.

"He stepped out," I said. "You want me to get him?"

"No," Ira said. "I wanted to make sure he was gone. I have to tell you something."

He lowered his voice the lowest I'd ever heard it. I put my ear right up to his mouth. "What?" I said.

"It wasn't an accident."

I turned my face to stare right at him. "Dillon," I said.

He closed his eyes.

"You said they would try to run you off the road." I was shaking my head. "But head-on?"

"It wasn't like that," he said. "I agreed to it."

"What do you mean you 'agreed to it'?" I said. "You were playing chicken on MaeAnne Boulevard?"

"No. It was a four-wheel drive contest. Up in the hills."

I stared at him.

"I thought if I scared them good, they would leave you alone. It fired."

"Fired?"

His eyes rolled back, and he fought them open. "Backfired," he said. "Dillon came right at me. I thought he would swerve off so I kept going. "

"And he didn't," I said.

"No."

"What is *wrong* with you, boy?" I said. "You're the one always telling me to 'calm down'—"

"These dudes are serious, baby."

"So am I!"

"If I hadn't done it, it would have been you." His eyes disappeared up into his head again, and his eyelids closed so hard I could have sworn I heard them slam.

"Ira?" I whispered. Pain flared up in my chest. "Honey?"

I clutched the side of the gurney with my whole heart right up in my throat. But his breathing was deep and heavy. All I could do was watch him lie there like a doll somebody had thrown against a wall and wish he would open his eyes one more time.

I don't know how long it was before I heard the curtains scrape open and felt Dr. Quao at my elbow.

"He's out," he said quietly.

"I want to have a few minutes alone with him," somebody else said in a cold voice. "Before they take him up to surgery."

I jerked my head up. Mrs. Quao looked down at me from her queenly height, eyes glittering.

"Why don't you go think about why this happened?" she said. "And I mean think hard."

Dr. Quao squeezed my arm, and I looked at him. My chest was heaving.

He nodded to me, and of course he closed his eyes and smiled. I found my way out of the ER in a blur.

In the waiting room, Koretta was curled up on the couch with her head in Mama's lap. Mama held out her arm to me when she saw me.

"What, baby?" she said.

"I don't know," I said. "Winnie just threw me out of there like I was the dirty laundry."

"I know what this is like for her," Mama said. "You do, too. She's so upset she can't think straight—"

"Oh, I'm thinking plenty straight."

I turned around to face Mrs. Quao, practically nose to nose. She didn't look upset to me. She looked like she wanted to strangle me with the sleeve of her designer workout jacket. She drilled her eyes into me.

"This isn't Oakland, Brianna," she said. "We don't live like that here."

"I know it," I said. "We don't either."

"Don't you?"

I shook my head, but I have to admit, I was itching to tell her exactly what I thought. Wherever she was going with this, I wasn't going to that place without a fight.

"Then why was Ira up in the hills, getting himself run down by a gang of white boys?" she said.

"Are you saying that was my fault?" I said.

"Who else's? Ira has been raised in a nonviolent home. We don't solve our problems by trying to run someone off the side of a mountain."

"And you think I do?"

"I think this never would have happened if Ira weren't in this relationship with you."

The woman's eyes were as cold and hard as a pair of diamonds. The only thing that was going to cut them was another pair, just as cold and hard. My mother hurled herself off the couch, leaving Koretta's head flopping, and stared right into Winnie Quao's face.

"Now just what do you mean by that?" Mama said.

"Mama—"

"No, Brianna. I want to know. What are you saying, Winnie?"

Mrs. Quao drew herself up like some kind of indignant exclamation point and glared down at my mother. "I'll tell you exactly what I'm saying. Ira was brought up to respect himself and know that he is every bit as good as, if not superior to, any white boy. He knows better than to stir up trouble and get himself mixed up in some kind of low-class, no-count gang fight. And until he started seeing her, it never would have entered his mind. Now he's been dragged down like some Oakland street kid. Who else am I going to blame but this girl?"

"'This girl'?" Mama said. "You're speaking of my Brianna?"

"That is *exactly* who I'm talking about, and you know it."

"Ex*cuse* me?"

"That's right! I've told Saban since the beginning that she was no good for Ira—"

"I cannot believe I'm hearing this."

"You *better* believe it, 'cause I'm gonna tell you what—"

Their voices rose and tangled like the wails of two cats in an alley, Mama's tightening into her most correct English and

Winnie Quao's dropping into the Southern black vernacular she had stuffed somewhere when she married a doctor. I left them sharpening their claws and fled for the door. It slapped open at my step, and I plunged out. The snappy March night stung at my face as I searched for a telephone.

A pay phone was located in the glare of the emergency room sign. I headed for it, digging in my purse for a quarter and groping in my head for Tobey's phone number.

I was acting more from reflex than actual thought as I stabbed my fingers at the buttons on the phone. I was shaking, and my mind couldn't hold on to a thought. My heart was pounding at every pulse point till I thought I'd explode. Tobey would get me calmed down. She was the one to call at a time like this.

But she wasn't home. I hung up when the answering machine started.

My ears were hammering as I pawed in my bag for another quarter. Ira's mother was blaming me. That was all I could think of, and I needed to hear the voice of somebody sane before I started to believe it myself.

I tried Norie's, but I hung up after three rings. If she had been home, she would have been studying right next to her phone. She was probably at Wyatt's. I didn't know his number.

I reinserted the quarter and strained to think. I knew Cheyenne's, but much as I loved that girl, she would either want to bring Diesel down here to kick some tail or she would give me twenty minutes worth of what I ought to tell that Mrs. Queen or Quota or whatever her name was. What I needed was somebody to talk me out of doing that.

I groped around in my purse some more and took out my little address book. Folded up in the back was the sheet Norie had made up for us back in September so we could call each other if we ever needed to. I'd never used it much.

I'd never needed to before.

The only two left were Shannon and Marissa. Shannon could at least listen. Maybe I could just vent to her.

I know I wasn't even thinking straight as I punched out her number and clung to the phone wire. Ira was in there being cut open in the operating room. His mother and mine were having a catfight in the waiting room. And I was calling a porcelain doll to talk me out of taking out my nail file and threatening everybody with it.

"Hello?" said a staccato male voice.

"Hello, this is Brianna Estes," I said. "May I speak with Shannon please?"

There was a sharp silence on the other end.

"*Who* is this?" he said.

"Brianna Estes," I said.

"You're a friend of Shannon's?"

"Yes," I said.

Did he think I was some kind of telemarketer or something? I shifted impatiently against the phone shell.

"Is she home?" I said.

"She can't come to the phone," he said.

He didn't ask if I wanted to leave a message. I didn't offer. I hung up and stared at the sheet of numbers.

Marissa.

The girl would probably faint the minute I started to talk. I folded up the paper to stick it back into my purse. That's when I saw how bad my hands were shaking. I could barely open the zipper.

"Lord, have mercy," I murmured. Glancing once more at the sheet, I poked out Marissa's number. She answered on the second ring.

"Hey, girl," I said. "This is Brianna."

"Oh . . . hi!" she said.

I didn't blame her for sounding surprised. When the Flagpole Girls met I forgot she was there half the time, she was so quiet. Who would have thought I'd ever call her?

"I'm at St. Mary's," I said.

I could hear her gasping.

"It's Ira," I said. "He was in an accident. Well, not really an accident. You remember those skinheads at the Jack-in-the-Box?"

"Yeah."

"They were all four-wheeling up in the hills, and one of them rammed into Ira head-on. He's going into surgery."

"My gosh!" she said. "Is he going to be okay?" Her voice was already shaking worse than mine.

"He's going to be fine," I said. "His father says he doesn't think Ira has any internal injuries. A neck fracture—"

"He has a broken *neck?*" Marissa said.

"Yes, but you know—"

"Brianna, that's awful! He could be paralyzed!"

"No, girl, he's gonna be all right. He's getting the best care. His daddy isn't going to allow anything else."

"Those guys *are* dangerous, just like you said."

"One of them's not," I said. "Not now. Dillon's banged up as bad as Ira. We won't have to worry about him for a while . . ."

My voice trailed off. I'd called for some strength, and I was the one doing the calming down. I could hear Marissa breathing like some kind of train on the other end.

"It's gonna be all right," I said.

"I'm so sorry," she said.

"Listen, I have to go. I'll see you tomorrow."

"Okay . . . well . . . 'bye."

I hung up the phone, but I held on to the receiver and put my head on my hand. I might as well have been standing on a street corner in the middle of Moscow asking for directions. Not one, single person understood what I needed.

I gave the receiver a final squeeze and turned out of the phone shell.

Two steps away a kid was standing there, glaring at me with stone eyes from out of the black hood of his sweatshirt.

I made a U-turn and headed the other way. He planted himself in front of me like a lanky toad springing out from under a rock.

"Let me by," I said.

"No," he said in a hollow voice. "I got something to say to you."

CHAPTER
FIVE

GARRICK BYERS WAS THE SMALLEST OF VAN'S TRIO,
but he might as well have been Charles Manson, hard as I was
shaking. Plus, his eyes were narrowed in on me like darts.
Poison darts.

I willed my lips to stop shivering, and I tried to push past
him. He stood in my path and gave me a shove with his fore-
arm, right in the collarbone. I stumbled back against the
hedge along the windows. He might have been the runt, but
he was wiry. My chest throbbed, enough to keep me from
coming right back at him with my fingernails out. As it was,
I just regained my balance and tried to outstare him.

He wasn't going to waver that easily.

"All right, *what?*" I said. My voice was about the only
thing on me that wasn't shaking—thank God.

"Your boyfriend messed way up," Garrick said.

"So did yours," I said.

"You think you're all bad, but that isn't gonna help you
this time."

"I'm quaking in my pumps," I said. "You done?"

He shook his head. I kept my gaze locked in. His eyes
weren't as marijuana-murky as Dillon's or Van's, but the left
one had a weird twitch to it. I stared at it, trying to get him to
go self-conscious. He just kept looking at me.

"So? *What?*" I said. "Whatever it is you have to say, go on
and say it. I got to go check on Ira."

"What about Dillon?" he said.

"What about him?"

"You gonna check on him—seein' how your boyfriend tried to kill him?"

"I heard it was the other way around," I said. "Matter of fact, I know it was because I was standing right there when Van started this whole thing. Ira doesn't pick fights."

"He challenged us."

"Liar!"

"He did! He stood there with his chest all puffed out the way you coons do and said he knew how to settle it."

Garrick took a step toward me, so close I could smell the stench of tobacco on his breath. I didn't move. I stood there acting like I didn't have a seven-piece drum kit jamming in my ears.

"You are a lying sack of fertilizer, boy," I said. "Van was out to get Ira, and he got him, simple as that. If Van wasn't so stupid, he could have figured out how to do it without getting his own guy, too."

Garrick blinked, and for a hair-width of a second, his eyes wavered away from mine. "Dillon could die," he said.

Another half-second and he was a lost, begging little boy standing in front of me. Another, and his eyes tightened back into points. It was enough though.

I stepped back from him and put my hands on my hips. "Boy, we can stand here and talk about this until we both freeze off our tails, but you and I know what the truth is so I really don't see the point. I'm going back inside, and I'm waiting to hear about Ira. You go on back to Van and tell him nice try, but if anybody goes down, it's gonna be—"

I stopped. What the heck was I doing?

"What?" Garrick said. He was pulling his face in sharper and hitching his shoulders.

"Just tell him I'm sorry about Dillon," I said. "And I wish this whole thing never happened."

Whether Garrick knew I meant it, I couldn't tell. I didn't

wait to find out. In the moment that he was caught off guard, I headed down the sidewalk and slid in with a knot of people who were going for the front door. When I looked back, he was running toward the parking lot.

Mean as a snake as Ira's mother was acting, she had to be easier to handle than the skinheads when they had somebody under the surgeon's knife. Garrick was obviously going for re-inforcements. I headed for the waiting room.

Mama, Winnie Quao, and Koretta were all sitting on the couch, and Dr. Quao was standing in front of them, hands folded against his stomach, head nodding as he talked. When I came up beside him, he put his arm around me. I kept my eyes away from Mrs. Quao.

"We've had word," he said to me. "Things are going nicely."

"How much longer?" I said.

"Hours!" Koretta said. Did that girl love to be the bearer of bad news or what?

I looked at Mama, and she held her arms out to me. I sat on the floor in front of her and put my head in her lap. She stroked my head. I could hear Winnie Quao making a *T* sound with her tongue.

"Come," Dr. Quao said to her. "We'll take a walk."

His voice was so calm, so quiet. Just like Ira's.

"Are you all right, baby?" Mama said as Dr. and Mrs. Quao left the room.

I just nodded. I knew if I talked I'd cry. And Brianna Estes did not cry.

So we sat there in silence, the three of us. Koretta whim-pered every now and then, all curled up at one end of the couch with a Kleenex up to her mouth. Mama patted her knee, but I could tell even my mother was about fed up. I was sure she was thinking, *Get a grip, girl, this is surgery, not a funeral.*

Still, the quiet was about to drive me wild. I couldn't stand the sound of my own thoughts, pounding in my head right along with my heartbeat.

"I'm just thinking about how to keep you out of trouble." That's what Ira had said. And Winnie: *"I think this never would have happened if Ira weren't in this relationship with you."* Then that shaved-headed little punk: *"Ira challenged us."*

I stood up and walked over to the water fountain, pretending to need a drink. They were wrong, all of them. That wasn't the way it went down. It wasn't my fault.

It *wasn't.*

I had to struggle to swallow a mouthful of water. When Norie appeared around the corner, I was never so happy to see somebody. Neither one of us was into hugging, but we flew at each other. Over Norie's shoulder I saw Tobey, and I let go and plastered myself against her.

"How did you know?" I said.

"Marissa called me at Wyatt's," Norie said.

"No way," I said.

Tobey gave me a big-eyed look and nodded her head a little. Marissa was hugging the wall.

"Was it all right that I called them?" she said. "I didn't know what else to do."

"Yes, girl! They were the ones I wanted in the first place—"

I didn't know what I was saying. Tobey grabbed me by the arm and got me to a chair before I could push my foot any farther into my mouth.

"How about Cokes for y'all?" Mama said. "I'm making a trip down to the cafeteria."

Everyone muttered thanks, and I sank back into the chair and closed my eyes as Mama left.

"What happened?" Norie said. "Marissa told us the skinheads rammed Ira four-wheeling?"

I nodded.

"What the heck was he doing up there with them?" Tobey said. "They must have followed him—"

"Oh, come on," Norie said. "Ira wouldn't go four-wheeling by himself. Unless he's an idiot."

Tobey jabbed her with an elbow.

"Which we all know he isn't," Norie added.

"I don't get it," Marissa said.

"It was a contest," I said.

"Like, somebody challenged somebody?" Norie said.

"Those animals." Tobey squeezed my hand. "You knew they were bad news, Brianna. You said it."

I glanced around the waiting room. Koretta had her eyes closed, and she had stopped whimpering. The rest of the place was empty. I lowered my voice anyway.

"Garrick was stalking me outside when I went to use the phone," I said.

Marissa gasped.

"He said Ira challenged *them.*"

"No way!" Tobey said.

"What else is he going to say?" Norie said. "First, Van told him to say that, and second, you really think they're going to admit *they* did anything wrong? The superior, Aryan race? Jackals."

Tobey blinked at me. "You didn't believe that scumbag, did you? Come on, Brianna, Ira is way too cool to lower himself to something like that."

I poked up my chin. "I know. You don't have to tell me that."

"So what do we do?" We all looked at Marissa. She was folding and unfolding her hands like they were napkins she couldn't get right.

"About what?" I said.

"Just . . . to help you?"

The three of them looked at me—three wholesome, open faces, three pairs of bright brown eyes, three heads of straight, silky hair.

I put my head down and rubbed the back of my neck with

both hands. Why was all *that* going through my head? I wanted them here. I wanted them to pray with me. But all of a sudden they looked like three little white angels in a dark place they couldn't understand.

"Let's just pray," I said. "Ira told me this afternoon, 'This isn't over.' He's right. We need strength."

"Ms. Race said be careful what you pray for," Tobey said.

"Well, Ms. Race isn't me, now, is she?" I said.

I bowed my head and reached out for hands. I could feel them all looking at each other. I had a wild thought that maybe I should have called Eden or Laraine instead.

We prayed though, and Mama came in with Cokes. We drank them and the Girls left.

"You call me if you need anything," Norie said as they were going. "Doesn't matter if it's the middle of the night. I have my own line."

"Okay," I said. But I knew I wouldn't. I just needed Ira to come out of surgery and tell me what to do. If he didn't, I was flat out going to die.

I thought that thought over and over again after the Girls left and the Quaos came back. We all sat in stiff silence, watching the door. I got to the point after two hours that, if I had to think that thought one more time, I was going to start ripping out-of-date magazines apart. Only the appearance of a man in green from head to toe saved an ancient *People* from becoming confetti.

Koretta started to whine, and Mrs. Quao moved across the floor like a crazed goose. The surgeon looked over both their heads at Dr. Quao.

"He came through it fine," he said. Then he spewed out a string of words a yardstick long that Dr. Quao nodded at for a solid three minutes. Winnie nodded, too, as if she understood every word he was saying.

Finally I couldn't deal with it anymore. "Just tell us if he's going to be all right!" I said.

The surgeon looked at me like I was invisible, and Dr. Quao smiled and patted my arm.

"He is," he said. "But it's going to be a long journey. Traction. Physical therapy. Patience."

"How long?" I said.

"Before he's on his feet? Three months?" He looked at the surgeon who was already backing toward the door.

"At least," he said. "We'll know more when he's fully conscious. Tomorrow afternoon at the earliest."

Mrs. Quao sagged against her husband, and Koretta ran to them and burrowed her head in her father's chest. Mama put her arm around me, and we stood there like two pitiful birds watching them hold each other up.

Dr. Quao lifted his head and smiled at me. "We must all pull together for Ira," he said.

"Right," I said. "We'll pull together."

But I felt about as together with anybody as a hawk on a telephone line.

I slept a total of three hours that night. And Mama drove me to school the next day before hurrying off to work.

"This is too far out of your way," I told her. "I could take the bus."

"You could not. You would fall right over in the aisle," she said. She pulled up in front of the school and looked at me. "You sure you're going to be all right, baby?"

The lines around her eyes and mouth were etched in sharper than ever today, and she wasn't smiling. She looked like a fifty-year-old woman—or a thirty-seven-year-old who hadn't slept all night. It pulled at me.

"I'm fine, Mama," I said.

"Don't you lie to me, girl-child."

"No, I am!"

"You don't believe any of that mess Winnie Quao was talkin', now, do you?"

"No," I said. "Ira makes his own decisions. I don't know *what* was up with that."

Behind us somebody blew a horn, and she ignored it. "I didn't want to ask you this last night. I mean, we were all upset."

"Mama, I have to go," I said. "I'm going to be late, and somebody's going to run *you* off the road, if you don't get out of the way."

I pecked her cheek with my lips and got out of the car.

"We'll talk tonight," she said.

"Uh-huh," I said.

Then I practically ran up the steps before she could park the car and come after me to ask me any more questions. It was one thing to keep stuff from Mama to protect her. She came to Reno to get away from the violence and the fear, and the less she knew about what brought on the accident the better. But it was a whole other thing to lie to her. I didn't lie to Mama.

The last bell was about to ring when I reached my locker, but Cheyenne was waiting there for me like she had all day to get to class.

I went into my usual Cheyenne-mode. "What are you doing, girl?" I said. "You want to start living in detention again?"

"I don't care about that!" she said fiercely. "Are you okay?"

I stopped with my hand on my lock.

"You heard," I said.

"Fletcher told me. Why didn't you call me? I'd have been right over there."

I wish I had now, I thought. *I'd have set you on Mrs. Quao. She wouldn't know what to do with you.*

"I'm all right," I said instead. "And Ira's going to make it."

"What about that other kid?"

"I don't know."

Cheyenne leaned in so close I almost slammed her head in the locker.

"I know it's not Christian to say this," she whispered, "but I almost hope he dies."

"Cheyenne Jackson, that is nasty!"

"I know. That's why I didn't say it out loud."

"Don't say it any way. Don't even think it."

"Don't you kind of wish it, too, though? I mean, for real?"

"No, I do not! Now you just hush up about that. Matter of fact, don't even talk about this to anybody, you hear?"

Cheyenne blew up at her bangs. "Why not?"

"Because I don't want any trouble."

"How can you say that?" She shifted her backpack and scurried off after me down the hall as the bell went off. "Aren't you ticked off about Ira? Don't you want to get back at those jerks?"

I grabbed her by the backpack strap and brought her up to my face. "Why do you come to the Flagpole group, girl?"

"What do you mean? You guys are my friends—my family."

"Why?"

"Because we're all Christians. We have to stick together."

"And can you see Jesus Christ saying, 'Let's get back at those jerks for hurting Ira'?"

"Well, no. But see, Jesus didn't have to worry about these bigots. I mean, He was white and so was everybody else, Peter and all those guys, so—"

"Girl, you do not know what you are talking about." I let go of her. "Get to class."

"See you at lunch?"

"No," I said. "I'll call you later."

I'd already thought about lunch when I was getting dressed that morning. I knew I better get myself to the Box and calm Eden and Laraine and the rest of them down. I had visions of them hiding in their lockers right now, waiting for me to tell them what to do next.

"Like I know," I muttered to myself.

The hall was empty, and all the classroom doors were closed as I half-ran toward my room near the outside door. Mr. Lowe was probably looking suspiciously at his grade book since Ira and I both hadn't shown up. He gave me enough dirty looks as it was because I talked to Ira all the time in class.

"Seymour, you and Charlotte Ann need to get to work back there," he would say.

I never asked him who Seymour and Charlotte Ann were. Nor did I tell him that we weren't just flapping our lips. I was helping Ira. The boy couldn't spell worth beans.

I reached for the doorknob now and listened. Mr. Lowe was already going on about Hamlet. He got so into it, maybe he wouldn't stop and give me one of those squinty-eyed looks through his glasses when I came in.

I turned the knob, and then my arm was jerked, and somebody was hissing hot breath in my ear. "We got something to discuss first," he said.

With his fingers wrapped like steel bands around my arm, Van Hessler dragged me through the door to the outside.

CHAPTER SIX

THE ICY OUTDOOR AIR HIT ME LIKE A SLAP IN THE face. But nothing could have been colder than Van's eyes freezing right into mine. They were close. His ugly mouth was close. The odor of his clothes, his cigarettes, and his dope made me nauseous.

I tried to pull away, but he held on hard, like one of those finger puzzles that gets tighter the more you try to wriggle out of it. I stood still and stared back at him, but my chest was thundering.

"Your boyfriend couldn't handle it," he said. "And the rest of you can't either."

"Handle what?" I said.

"Us."

He hissed out the s, and I flared my nostrils at him. Even his voice stunk. "You only think you're tough, but we took him out, and we'll take you, too. All of you."

"For what?" I said.

"For bein' black," he said. "That's for openers. And for Dillon."

I felt my first real flicker of fear. "How is he?" I said.

"He's in a coma. You oughta go see him. So you'll know what it looks like to be lyin' there like some thing in a bed."

"You don't have anyone to blame but yourself. Ira's not much better off, and you don't hear me threatening—"

"I'm not threatening," he said. "I'm promising."

"Ooh," I said. "I'm afraid."

He yanked so hard on my arm my head went back and my teeth clacked together. His fingers dug into my flesh.

"Let go," I said. I kept my lips stiff. It sounded tough—and it kept my mouth from trembling. It was cold and I was scared and so full of hate I wanted to bite something.

"Be afraid," he said. "Be very afraid. Dillon took the risk, and I'll take it, too. Whatever it takes to get your stinkin' kind out of here."

He used filthier words I've tried to block out, without much success. They burned right down through my ears and branded themselves inside me.

"Let go, or I'm going to scream," I said. "I mean it."

"You just get out while you still can," he said. He gave my arm one more jerk and then turned me loose.

I didn't wait to watch him go. Pulling open the door, I threw myself back into the hall. Warm air bit at my numb fingers, but I was cold from the inside out.

I passed my classroom, all the classrooms, and found my way to the girls' rest room on the corner. Somebody—a big blob of a person—was standing at the sink, but I didn't even look at her as I slammed into one of the stalls and leaned my forehead against the metal on the closed door.

Dillon took the risk. He plowed his vehicle head-on into Ira on purpose. That was how much he despised us.

For being black.

There is no cold like hate-cold. I pulled my arms around myself, and I stood in that stall, and I shook. Who knows how long I would have stayed, trembling like I had the palsy, if I hadn't heard somebody say, "Brianna? Where are you?"

It was Cheyenne. I flattened myself against the door.

"In there," another, gruffer voice said. That was Cheyenne's foster sister Felise. She talked like a truck driver. She must have been the blob at the sink, and she must have gotten Cheyenne.

Cheyenne pulled on the handle from the outside. "Brianna? What's going on? Come out."

"Go away, Cheyenne," I said. "I'm using the bathroom."

"For ten minutes? Come on, open up."

"Get on back to class, girl. Can't a person use the john in private?"

Evidently not. Cheyenne gave up on the door. Next thing I knew, her head was coming up over the side of the stall.

"What are you doing?" I said.

"I'm standing on the toilet. What's going on? What are you doing in here? Did Mr. Lowe yell at you for being late? Man, there's no compassion anymore, you know that? These teachers, what, do they have to check in their hearts at the front desk when they get here in the morning? Didn't you tell him what was going on with Ira and everything?" She stopped—thankfully—and craned her neck at me.

"Brianna, you look terrible," she said. "Come on, what happened? You're scaring me."

I sank down on the edge of the toilet and pulled up the sleeve of my sweater. Angry purple welts stared up at me.

"Whoa," Cheyenne said. "What happened?"

All I could do was stare back at my arm. *Dillon took the risk. I'll take it, too. Whatever it takes to get your stinkin' kind out of here.*

"I'm getting the Girls together," she said. "You meet us at lunch; I mean it, Brianna."

I jerked my head up at her. "Who do you think you're talking to, girl?"

"I'm talking to you just the way you would talk to me if this was reversed. You've locked yourself in the bathroom. I might be in the dumb classes, but I'm not totally stupid. You need help. Now come on, come out of there. I'll get the Girls together, and we'll figure something out."

"You can't figure this out," I said. "Nobody can figure this out."

"Fine," she said. "I'll tell that to *God* next time we talk."

I tried to wither her with a black look. She kept hanging over the side of the stall, giving me an even blacker one.

"We'll pray," she said. "It always works out when we pray. Think about it—with Tobey, then Norie, then even me. I'd probably be back in Wittenberg right now if it weren't for us all getting together and praying and doing a Plan—"

"Cheyenne—"

"I know you're going to say I'm naive, and I don't know diddly and all that, but I do know. *You* taught me."

I closed my eyes, but I could still see her waiting.

"If I say yes, will you shut up?" I said.

"Yeah," she said.

"Then okay."

"You'll be there?"

"Yes."

"I'll meet you outside the art room, and we'll walk over together."

"I'll *be* there."

She still peered at me like a condor for another ten seconds before she climbed down off the toilet and clambered out of the restroom with Felise. I waited until they were well down the hall before I came out and looked at myself in the mirror. I let my lips go, and they shook. When I put my hands up to my cheeks, they were trembling, too. I wondered if anybody had ever watched herself have a nervous breakdown before.

I'm just going to fall apart, I thought. *I'm just going to stand here and go right to pieces on the floor.*

Fine, Cheyenne would have said. *I'll tell God that next time we talk.*

It made me want to laugh. She had sounded like me. That was something I would have said to her, if, like she said, the situation had been reversed. The little runt.

But it was enough to get me out of the bathroom and down the hall to Mr. Lowe's room. I barely heard him when he asked for the pass I didn't have, and whatever he said about Hamlet I was going to have to catch some other time. All I could do to keep my face from shaking was think about Cheyenne saying, "I'll tell God that next time we talk."

Okay, the Girls could help me pray. And that afternoon Ira would know what to do. He would tell me what to do. It could be okay.

No, it was never going to be okay—

Fine, I'll tell God that next time we talk.

I went through that same cycle at least fifty times through English and government. By the time I got to the first of my two back-to-back art classes, I could see some hope. A glimmer.

Still, after Ms. Squires gave the drawing assignment and everybody started to work, I stared at the blank piece of paper in front of me for a good five minutes. Then I realized I hadn't even heard what we were supposed to do.

"Nice work," Ms. Squires said dryly behind me. She had sarcasm down to an art form. I'd seen little freshman girls reduced to tears by it.

"Tell me you're not burned out," she said.

"No," I said.

"Swept away by success?"

I looked up at her sharply. She had a little square gleam in her beady, blue eyes. That was about as close as she ever came to a grin.

"What do you mean?" I said.

She folded her arms across her chest, currently covered with a paint-spattered, neon green sweater, and held her head back the way she did when she was observing a drawing. Her hair-the-color-of-dried-sage threatened to fall out of the knot she had made with it on top of her head. Not surprising since it was only being held in place with a pencil.

"I've been hearing some pretty positive feedback on your show."

Whoa. I'd almost forgotten about it. Yesterday morning seemed like a hundred years ago.

"I just wondered if you figure you've peaked," she said.

"That would be depressing," I said. "Thinking there's nothing beyond this."

"Tell me about it."

She reached down and picked up my blank piece of paper.

"Let it go for today," she said. "Wallow in your ego for the next two periods. We'll pick it up again tomorrow."

I know my mouth was hanging open as I watched her sway on down the table, with her long, muslin skirt rocking back and forth across her hips and black Converse tennis shoes flapping on the linoleum.

"That woman is a trip," Ira said to me about three times a week.

Ira.

He said so many cool, gentle, and good things to me. I missed him. If anything happened to him—

I couldn't think about that.

I folded my arms on the table and put down my head.

"So how come you get to sleep?" somebody said.

I raised up enough to look at the girl across the table. She didn't usually sit there, but she sure was taking an interest in me now. She had these gravel-colored eyes, which were boring into me from between two panels of limp, colored-too-many-times black hair. Her skin was as pale as Shannon's. Her dark red lipstick against it made her look like Morticia Addams.

"Why can't the rest of us take a nap?" she said.

Ordinarily I'd have told her "the rest of you" didn't open a one-woman art show in the library with twenty paintings you've been working on for five months. But I didn't feel like it that day. Besides, what was it to her? I'd barely noticed she was in our class except to hear her whining when we critiqued her drawings, which a four-year-old with no thumbs could have done.

"You have a problem with it, go talk to Ms. Squires," I said.

I put my head back down.

"Didn't get much sleep last night, huh?" the girl said.

I didn't answer.

"Neither did I. You know why?"

Her voice was starting to grate on me. It had a rough texture to it, like she had sand in her throat.

"Hey, do you know why?" she said again.

"Rachel, why are you at that table?" Ms. Squires said.

"Why can't I sit here?"

"Because you're annoying," Ms. Squires answered.

"Could you be any more rude?" Rachel said.

"Definitely. But you don't want that. Now move."

I grinned into my arms. I'd never realized that I liked Ms. Squires quite that much. That was two points for her today.

I could hear Rachel's chair scraping back as she moved. Something picked at the edges of my arms, and I looked up. She had left a piece of paper there, touching me.

I glanced at it and started to put my head back down, but the letters scrawled across it screamed at me, and I stared at it.

"Black witch," it said. A childish cartoon drawing of a figure with enormous lips and a cap of kinky hair looked up at me. There was a bone through its nose.

I picked up the sheet, folded it in half, and slowly, methodically tore it into tiny pieces. I could feel Rachel's eyes on my back as I neatly pushed the pile aside and put my head down on my arms. I could feel the welts under my sweater. And it all hurt.

TRUE TO HER WORD, CHEYENNE WAS WAITING OUT-
side the art room when the bell rang for lunch.

"What did you do, girl?" I said. "Sneak out before the end
of fourth period?"

"I'm not giving away my tricks," she said. She tucked her
arm through mine like she was afraid I was going to bolt and
dragged me toward the theater lobby.

"I'm coming," I said. "You don't have to haul me like the
chain gang."

"Did you ever have any ancestors in chains?" she said.

"What?" I said.

"Were any of your ancestors slaves? You know, like on a
plantation?"

I shook my head at her. "You are a trip, girl."

That was what Ira would have said. I must have been ex-
periencing shock or something, because every time I thought
about him, I started to shake again. I gripped Cheyenne's
arm.

"Don't worry," she whispered to me. "We'll fix this."

All the Girls were there except Ms. Race, which, for some
reason I couldn't quite put my finger on, was fine with me.

"I hope it's okay that I didn't invite the boys," Norie said
to me as I joined them on the cold tiles in our corner of the
lobby.

Sometimes we invited Diesel, Fletcher, Ira, and Wyatt.

And sometimes we chose not to. Right now, I wasn't sure it mattered one way or the other.

Next to me, Shannon was winding a piece of paper around her finger. It matched the one Marissa left lying on the floor while she opened her lunch.

Girls! (It read in the type font Norie always used.)

Emergency meeting in the theater lobby at lunch. Brianna has something major going down. With Ira in the hospital and Dillon's friends on the prowl, it goes without saying we'll all be there, right? IHS, Norie.

"What's 'IHS'?" Cheyenne said. "I Have Secrets?"

Tobey giggled. "I Have Snacks."

"Cool!" Cheyenne said. "What are they?"

"It's 'In His Spirit,' goofball," Norie said. She looked at me. "You look awful."

"Well, thank you," I said.

"I told you," Cheyenne said. "I thought she was totally going to hurl in the bathroom."

"Um, spare us the details," Shannon said. She put down her sandwich.

"Sorry," Cheyenne said.

Norie nudged me from across the circle with her foot. "So what's going on?"

"Cheyenne said you were wrecked," Tobey said.

"Like I said, she was about to puke," Cheyenne whispered to Shannon. Poor Shannon rewrapped her sandwich in the Saran and put it back in her lunch bag.

"We're ready to do whatever you need," Tobey said. "You know that."

I did know that, and I hoped my face was grateful as I looked at all of theirs. But as I watched them watching me and waiting, the same thing hit me that had the night before. Maybe because I'm an artist, the things I see tell a story to me. Their skin told me they had never been grabbed so hard it left welts. Their faces reflected an innocent world. Their straight, silky hair didn't know the rigors and the differentness of being black. How could they even hope to help me?

Something warm touched my hand. I looked down to see Marissa's fingers curling around mine. My eyes met hers in surprise. She pulled away and played with the straw in her juice box.

"Don't you clam up now," Cheyenne said. "If I didn't spill *my* guts, you would be all over me."

"Must we reduce everything to body waste?" Norie said to her.

"All right," I said. "I don't know what you can do about it, but here it is."

I told them what had happened with Van. They sat there, eyes getting bigger, faces getting less innocent. I felt worse after I'd told it. Until Tobey got up on her knees so she could look right in my face.

"You don't think we can help with that?" she said.

I shook my head.

"Then what are we here for?" she said. "We promised to be each other's Christian sisters and to be there whenever somebody needed us, not just when it was easy or it wasn't dangerous—"

"Or you couldn't end up getting your tires slashed or something," Norie said.

Tobey turned on her. "You don't think we should help?"

"I didn't say that. I'm just being realistic."

"I'd get my head blown off for you, Brianna," Cheyenne said.

"Um, is that for real?" Shannon said. "Would these guys really blow somebody's head off?"

"I was exaggerating," Norie said.

I wasn't sure she was. I wasn't sure about anything at the moment.

"But they don't play games," Norie added. "Look what happened to Ira."

"I don't care," Cheyenne said. She set her little shoulders. "I'm ready."

Shannon went back to playing with her meeting notice. I wouldn't have expected anything else. Matter of fact, she would be more of a liability than an asset if anything did go down . . .

Why are you thinking like this? I scolded myself. *You can't let any of them get involved in this.*

"I'm confused," Marissa said.

"Why?" Norie said.

"What is it we're talking about doing?"

They all looked at each other, and I groaned inside. This was about pointless.

"I don't think we know yet," Tobey said finally. "I guess Brianna tells us what she needs, and then we pray and let God tell us how to do it. Isn't that the way we usually operate?"

"But this isn't like usual," I said. "We're not talking about cheating or shoplifting. This is people's lives, and I don't think—"

"You dealt pretty well with my life, when that whole thing went down with Coach," Tobey said. "I wouldn't have had a friend left in this school if it hadn't been for you guys. That's life, if you ask me." Her face had lost its sunniness. She was serious as a judge.

"I'd say we pretty much saved Cheyenne's, too," Norie said. "I mean, she could have gone to Wittenberg for shoplifting. What's different about you that you can't accept our help?"

They all looked at me. For the first time since September, when we had all met each other on See You at the Pole Day, I did feel different from them. I could see the scene in my mind. All of them with their clear, white, simple problems. And me with my deep, black ones. I shook my head.

"That's the whole thing," I said. "I'm different. My situation is different. I don't see how you can help, except pray for me so Ira and I can figure something out and deal with it."

You would have thought I'd stepped right on their faces. I could see shoulders sagging all around the circle. Even Shannon's. Even Marissa's. The only person who seemed to like that decision was Ms. Race.

I don't know when she came in. She was still squatting behind me like she had just appeared. I knew for sure from the calm expression on her face that she hadn't heard about my encounter with Van Hessler.

"I'm liking the sound of that," she said. "I've told you before, some things are far too dangerous for you to try to handle alone."

"We're not exactly alone," Norie said. "I count six of us."

"I mean without adults," Ms. Race said. "Let's not mess with those guys down at the Jack-in-the-Box. We don't want any more people hurt. We can pray for protection, for healing for Ira."

She put her hand on my arm, right where Van had grabbed me. I tried not to wince.

"How is Ira?" she said. "What can we do for him?"

"Can we visit him?" Cheyenne said.

"Some of those Get Well balloons, maybe?" Shannon said.

It was all so naive, I wanted to laugh.

"I don't know anything," I said. "They won't know if there's going to be permanent damage until this afternoon."

"Waiting can be so hard," Ms. Race said.

They all looked at me sympathetically. I guess that was all they could do. But for the snapping-by of a moment, I actually resented them for it.

"Let's pray then," Tobey said. She didn't have the usual sparkle in her eyes as she took Norie's hand and Cheyenne's, and we all bowed our heads.

Tobey prayed for healing for Ira, and Norie put in her two cents about beefing me up for what was ahead. Ms. Race got in her thing about protection, and Cheyenne asked God to be sure "those jerks learned their lesson." Shannon murmured something under her breath. Marissa just squeezed my hand.

There was a strong "amen" and a group hug, but I didn't feel much of anything. That little glimmer of hope Cheyenne had given me was gone, and I just wanted to see Ira.

It took a few minutes to pick up all our lunch stuff while Cheyenne gave us an update on how many more days until spring break. Wyatt showed up to walk Norie to class, and Marissa and Shannon found Fletcher lurking by the garbage can and put their trash down his back. I stood there feeling lost. Ira was always around to walk to the next class with and run things by from the meeting and all that. It was so weird standing there alone. And then it got lonelier.

I had to pass Ms. Race when I crossed the lobby to the double doors to the hall. She was already in a conversation with Coach Gatney, and they were talking so deep, I had to wonder if it was about Ira and me. Silly me.

Just as I reached them, Coach Gatney said, "So you gave in and went out with him."

"I figured what did I have to worry about?" Ms. Race said. "What's going to happen in a restaurant in the middle of downtown Reno, right?"

"So, how did it go?"

Then Ms. Race giggled. She actually giggled.

That was what rode right between my shoulder blades, her acting all concerned about Ira and about my safety one minute, and then giggling over some dude the next—the very next. It gave me an ugly kind of loneliness, the kind you get when people are only pretending to care.

"Brianna?"

I stopped with my hand on the handle of the double door, but I didn't turn around. I sure didn't feel like talking to anybody.

Turns out I didn't have to. It was Marissa, and all she did was touch my sleeve like she was afraid of me and say, "Look, I know you get more support from Norie and Tobey. They're stronger like you, but I just wanted to say . . ."

She stopped as some impatient, eye-rolling people went

by. I wondered if she was going to say whatever she had on her mind after all, the way she was looking down the hall like all of a sudden she wanted to escape. I started to go on even, but she blurted it right on out. "I just wanted to say, I know what it's like to always have to explain who you are or defend it or something."

"You do," I said. It wasn't really a question. It was more like a statement I didn't believe.

"Yeah, I do," she said. Then she shrugged with her eyebrows and backed away. "I just wanted to say that," she said. She turned around and walked off.

So there I had it for support. A bunch of people who wanted to understand but couldn't. One who pretended to but wouldn't. And one who thought she did but didn't.

In computer typing, I logged on and went right to the drawing program. Let Mr. Cattlin say something to me because I wasn't practicing Microsoft Word. I was up for chewing somebody's head off. I started to draw something I didn't have to think about so I could pray on my own.

God, all I'm asking is that You let me have just one thing. Just let me have Ira awake and clear. Just let him tell me where to turn next, what road to go down, Lord. What direction to go.

I prayed and prayed and prayed, and then I looked at my screen. I'd drawn a clump of big signs, all shaped like fingers pointing down disappearing roads that went in all directions and met in a maze.

I hit delete and picked up my Microsoft Word manual.

That afternoon I waited for the city bus at the edge of the school parking lot. It would take me downtown, and then I could walk the five blocks to St. Mary's. I'd already called Mama, and she said she would pick me up there after work so we could go to dinner like we always did on Wednesday nights. I couldn't imagine eating a thing right now.

It was one of those go-right-through-you, March-windy days. The bus passed us to turn around at the end of the road, and I positioned myself to be first in line to board. I was about to freeze off my backside. Coming from the Bay area, I wasn't ever going to get used to this frosty-winded weather. As I stood there, a black Cherokee drove up and stopped at the curb, right where the bus would pull up.

I waved at the car's driver to move on about the same second I recognized the car. It was too late to turn away as the window on the passenger side rolled down. Garrick Byers stuck his head out the window.

"You still here, jungle bunny?" he said out of his ugly, nothing-more-than-a-hole mouth.

I decided to ignore him. The motor revved impatiently.

"You deaf?" he said.

I still didn't answer. I watched the bus barrel toward us.

"That was a good move staying away from the Jack-in-the-Box today," he said. "You're getting the idea."

I snapped my head toward him, just as the bus driver leaned on his horn. The Cherokee started to inch forward.

"Just keep making yourself invisible," Van said from the driver's seat. "The less we see you, the better off you'll be."

The bus horn blared again, and people started to jockey around me. The Cherokee squealed away from the curb and off down the road, barely missing a woman in an old Volkswagen turning the corner.

"Idiots," a guy behind me said.

I turned to agree. He looked at me like I wasn't there.

Just keep making yourself invisible, Van had said.

That shouldn't be too hard.

The only decent thing that happened all day was that Winnie Quao wasn't in Ira's room when I got there, and Ira was awake. I ran to him like a little girl. I hadn't felt that way probably ever. I buried my face into his cheek.

"Careful, baby," he said.

"Did I hurt you?"

"No, but I might hurt myself. Mmm-mmm. You look good."

I gazed into his swollen, purply face. "So do you," I lied.

He smiled about halfway.

So many tubes and lines, and bulky pieces of equipment surrounded him, there was only one place I could touch him and that was his cheekbone. I just kept stroking it. I felt young, scared, out of control.

He closed his eyes.

"Don't go to sleep on me," I said.

"No, I'm just feeling good. I'll give you about two hours to stop that."

"Or until you mother comes in," I said.

He opened his eyes, and they flickered at me through his drug-haze. "Koretta said my mom's been giving you a bad time."

"It doesn't bother me."

"It bothers me. I told Koretta to keep her off your back."

"It's all right. I can handle your mama." To prove it, I glanced back over my shoulder to be sure she wasn't there.

"Uh-huh," Ira said. "Well, there's something you're not handling. Talk to me, before she comes back."

I wanted to. I wanted to just spit out everything and let him fix it for me. I know twenty-four hours earlier I was telling him not to take care of me like I was some kind of child, but suddenly that was all I wanted him to do.

But he looked like he was hanging on to some kind of thread between him and pain. Breathing through a tube. Eating through a tube. Getting blood through a tube. There wasn't any more room for me to feed anything in.

"I'm just worried about you," I said. "Can you . . . ?"

No, I couldn't ask him that either. *So, Ira, can you move yet, or do you think you're going to be paralyzed for life like some kind of artichoke?*

"Baby, come on," he said. "I broke my neck, not my brain. It's still working."

"I know it. You don't have to tell me . . ."

"I wiggled my toes today. Okay, are you happy?"

I glared at him.

"Doctor says that's a good sign," Ira said. "Now will you please tell me what you're thinking before I have to get out of this bed and squeeze it out of you?"

"Uh-huh. You have three or four months before you do any squeezing, boy."

"Brianna, now."

I looked once more at the door and then at him. This really could be my last chance to talk to him for a while. I had to ask him, or I was all alone.

"I've been harassed by Van and Garrick," I said. "They've been making threats. I don't know if they're real or not."

Ira cringed. "How much more real do you want, baby?"

I looked at his IV bag. "Okay, so they mean it. I'll do whatever I have to. Just tell me how to fix it. Nobody else can."

I watched his face and waited for an answer. He couldn't move his head, but I could see him wanting to shake it.

"What?" I said. "What are you saying?"

"I'm saying I can't fix it. It's all up to you now, baby."

CHAPTER EIGHT

I STARED AT HIM FOR A GOOD FIFTEEN SECONDS. I was sure he was going to grin and say, "I was just playing with you, baby."

But he was far from playing. Doped up as he was, his eyes were clear-serious. I curled my fingers tight around the bars on his bed.

"What do you mean, it's up to me?" I said. "You couldn't handle those people; how do you expect me to do it without your telling me what to do?"

"You just said it. I couldn't handle them. I messed it up. How am I supposed to tell you what to do?"

"What would be your next move if you could get out of this bed right now?"

I could see him trying to swallow. "I don't have one."

"Well, you better think of one!" I said. I got my face close to his. "They are telling me to make myself invisible, Ira. They're saying the less they see of me, the better off I'll be. You want to see the welts on my arm from the last time Van Hessler 'saw' me?"

I shed my coat to the floor, jammed up my sweater's sleeve, and flung my arm right into Ira's face. He looked and closed his eyes. I pulled my arm away and shook my head.

"You open your eyes, Ira Quao, and you help me now.

Otherwise, I'm going to have to go into hiding—or get myself killed."

"They won't kill you."

"Why not? They tried to kill you!"

"They thought I'd back down."

"Uh-huh. And you didn't. Now they got somebody on death row."

"Death row?"

"Dillon is in a coma. He could die." My voice broke. I pulled my eyes into a line with my fingers to keep from crying. Brianna Estes does not cry. Ever.

"Okay, baby, okay," he said.

"Okay, what? What am I going to do, Ira?"

"You went to the Girls?"

"They're praying. What else are they going to do? Ms. Race wants me to run to the principal every time one of those skinheads looks at me cattywampus. You heard her yourself."

"I know."

"James and Harlan have gone into seclusion. I didn't see them all day."

"Does your Mama know?"

"No, she's been through enough. The minute I say I'm getting threats, she'll be moving me to North Dakota or somewhere."

"I'm thinking there is no place to run to."

"Then what am I going to do, Ira?"

I shook the bed, and Ira groaned. I stopped the bars and put my face down to his cheek. I was starting to shake again.

"I'm sorry," I said. "I'm sorry. I just can't hold it together much longer."

"I know," he said. His voice was its usual soft, but it was thready. I could hear the pain in it. "I'll get you some help."

Then he closed his eyes.

A pair of pumps tapped into the room. I didn't even have to turn around to know it was his mother. I could smell Clinique all the way from the doorway.

"Hi," I said.

She just nodded to me.

"He's sleeping," I said.

"I can see that," she said.

I shivered, and I left.

From the couch down in the lobby, I could see the circular driveway out front where Mama was going to pick me up. I curled into a ball on the end of it and kept my eyes glued to the window. She would be a good half-hour, but I wanted to get out of there. The smells, the sounds of the elevators and drug carts and that woman paging every doctor in life, it was all getting tangled up . . . Ira in his bed and Prentice, the way he had looked in his, and my daddy . . .

I squeezed my eyes shut. When I opened them, I told myself, this mess is going to be done.

I replaced it with what Ira had said. He was going to get me some help.

The only person I could imagine who could possibly help was Dr. Quao. I'd actually thought about him myself during the day. He knew, certainly, that Ira couldn't have just been in an accident. He was too smart a man not to have figured out something racial was involved. Why, he had told us stories himself of the prejudice he had had to deal with in medical school. He came from some kind of aristocratic family in Ghana, but here in the United States he had been treated like the custodian. Just last year, he had told us, he was at a medical conference in Chicago, walking through the hotel, and some white guy with a cigar hanging out of his mouth had whistled to him to carry his bags to the elevator.

But Dr. Quao had such faith that things were going to change. He believed in the institutions—the same way Ms. Race did. He would never hear of us putting down the school, the government, or the police. We had decided never to tell him about what happened with the police.

I had wanted to paint that scene ever since it happened because it was still so vivid in my mind. And so ugly.

Ira and I were going to a movie, but when he picked me up he realized he had forgotten his wallet at home.

"You'd leave your arm someplace if you could figure out how to get it off," I told him as we drove back down McCarran to Caughlin Boulevard.

"No, you would remind me," he said.

"I am not your mama," I said.

He grinned at me real big in the dusky half-light. "I know," he said.

I smacked him, and he got me around the neck and pulled me over so I sat real close to him. We were laughing and carrying on like we do. It was turning out to be one of those nights when everything was funny, and everything you did cracked you right up. Even when Ira looked in the rearview mirror and saw the cop car behind us, he said, "What did you do this time, girl? We got the police after us."

"It's you they want," I said as we turned into Ira's street. "You just look like a criminal."

That was a joke. He resembled a crook about as much as Denzel Washington. And street gangsters didn't live in Caughlin Ranch. His house was about as big as our apartment complex, and it was all dripping with crystal chandeliers and solid teakwood mantels and everything his mother could come up with to show the world she was oozing money.

"Whoever they're after is on my street," he said.

The words were barely out of his mouth when the blue lights started going. They reflected off the rearview and the side mirrors and set my eyes into the back of my head. They flashed across Ira's face as he pulled the truck over to the curb.

"They're stopping you?" I said.

"Looks like."

"You weren't going that fast," I said.

"I was going under the speed limit," he said. "I was trying to get them to go around me."

"Step out of the car," a voice said outside Ira's window.

Ira opened the window and leaned out.

"I'm sorry, sir," he said. "I'm on my way home to get my wallet. I don't have my license with me."

"I said, step out of the car!"

The cop's voice cut right into me. I touched Ira's arm.

"You keep your hands to yourself in there!" the cop barked.

On the other side of me, the passenger door opened, and the other officer said to me, "Step out and keep your hands away from your body."

She was a woman, but she talked like Bruce Willis in a *Die Hard* movie. I slid out and held my hands out stiffly to either side.

"Put them up on your head," she said.

I was so confused I didn't do it right away.

"Get them up!" she said. Or rather, screamed. I'd heard drug-addict mothers in East Oakland talk nicer to their kids.

"Now turn around and put your hands on the hood of the vehicle," she said.

I did, and I could see that the other policeman already had Ira flattened on the truck hood and was patting him down like he was beating a rug.

"What did we do?" I said.

"On the car!"

I made myself one with the truck and stayed stiff so I wouldn't shake. I wasn't going to give this chick the satisfaction of knowing I was about to wet my pants I was so scared. Luckily, my fingers accidentally touched Ira's, and I could feel that he was still warm. It helped.

The lady cop ran her hands over my body with about as much care as if she were checking her pockets before she put her jeans in the wash. Then she tugged at the back of my collar.

"Get up," she said.

I did.

Ira was already standing, and his officer moved him away so I couldn't hear them. That scared me, and when I get scared, as you know by now, I get mad.

"What is going on?" I said. "I think you're supposed to tell me."

"What were you doing driving in this neighborhood?" she said.

"Going to my boyfriend's house."

"Who's your boyfriend?"

I pointed to Ira. "Him. Ira Quao."

She started to smirk. With the lights blipping across her face, it made her look like something out of *Friday the Thirteenth.*

"He lives *here?*" she said. "In Caughlin Ranch?"

"Yes," I said.

"Where? Which house?"

I pointed three houses down where the Quao's driveway curved gracefully up from the street, behind the spiked wrought-iron fence.

"Right," she said. "So if we took you down there and knocked on the door, his mother would identify him?"

"No," I said. "She isn't home. Nobody's home."

"How convenient for you." She hissed out a laugh and looked over at the other cop. "What have you got?"

"Says he lives here."

"At least they got their stories straight."

"What 'stories'?" I said.

"I suggest you keep your mouth shut," she said to me. "Did you run the plates?"

"Just doing it," the other guy said.

I'd watched enough TV to know they were supposed to do that as soon as they started following. I guess when you're black, you don't get the same drill.

"Over there," the other officer said. He nodded his head abruptly for Ira to come and stand by the two of us. The woman stood between us, hand on her holster.

"What's going on, Ira?" I said.

"Let's just keep quiet," she said.

"I don't have to," I said. I didn't grow up in Oakland for nothing.

"You want me to cite you for—"

"Let's go up to the house and get that driver's license," the guy shouted to Ira.

The lady cop stared at the guy as he came up to Ira and jerked his head toward the Quaos' house.

"What?" she said.

"The plates match up with the address," the cop said to her between his teeth.

He and Ira booked on up to the house. The whole time they were gone I didn't even look at her. I didn't think I could stand it.

When they came back, that cop was in a hurry. He didn't look at anybody as he stomped on to the patrol car.

"*What?*" the woman said.

"He has a license; we can't hold 'em."

She swore and inserted herself into the car. Ira and I stood there and watched them make a U-turn and drive off.

"They didn't even apologize," Ira said.

I grunted. "You expected them to?"

We agreed not to tell his parents. Winnie would have gone ape, and Dr. Quao would have wanted to go through the proper channels to file a complaint. Ira said it just wasn't worth it. But after that he lost some of the gentleness he had inherited from his daddy. I said to him, "Welcome to my world, honey. That's what I grew up with."

Just thinking about it now made me feel all nettled and closed in. I got up and went outside. It was cold, but I'd rather shake from that than from my own thinking.

I'd only been sitting on the edge of a brick planter about five minutes when I saw four sets of legs coming across the driveway under a bouquet of Get Well balloons. I recognized Cheyenne's overalls.

"There's Brianna!" I heard her shout.

Tobey, Fletcher, and Marissa poked their heads out to the sides and grinned at me. They broke into a run, balloons bobbing all the way.

"Hey, girl!" Tobey said when they got to me. "We brought these for Ira. Just in case he could see us. I guess you figured that out; who else would they be for, right?" She giggled. Tobey only giggled like that when she was nervous. Her eyes were all over the place, too.

"He can have visitors," I said.

"Do you think he'll like them?" Marissa said.

I felt about an inch tall. I'd been so superior about how naive these white folks were. "They'll cheer him up," I said. "He needs cheering up."

"Is that bad?" Fletcher said. "I mean, you know, is he depressed because he . . . forget it."

"He's showing good signs," I said. I was starting to feel sorry for all of them. They looked like they would rather have their braces tightened than stand there wondering if they were making fools of themselves. "This was real nice of you," I said.

"It was Shannon's idea," Cheyenne said. "She wanted to come bad. She got us to take her to Safeway to buy the stuff and everything, but when her dad found out, he wouldn't let her come. I didn't know he was like that, but he—"

"Cheyenne, stick one of these balloons in your mouth, would you?" Tobey said.

Cheyenne looked bewildered, and Fletcher whispered in her ear. I turned to Marissa. "Well, thanks. He has a bunch of fussy flowers up there, but nothing like this."

She looked like I'd just gotten her off a bum rap. Tobey grinned again, too.

"So, how did you get here?" she said.

"Bus."

"You're going home on the bus, too?" That thought obviously blew her away. You would have thought I'd hitchhiked from Canada.

"My mama's coming for me," I said.

"I like how you call her your 'mama.'" Cheyenne said. "Is that a black thing?"

"From now on, I'm bringing you over here after school," Tobey said. "Riding the bus is too dangerous. People are always getting their stuff stolen or being offered drugs on there." She shuddered.

I grunted.

"Is that her coming?" Marissa said, pointing to our rattle-trap Ford.

Huh. They had never even met Mama. None of them had ever been to our apartment. They didn't know I took the bus all over town.

I'd thought the Flagpole Girls were my close friends. Turns out, as Cheyenne would say, they didn't know diddly about my life.

It felt comforting to get into the car with Mama. She had Aretha Franklin in the tape player. "Respect" was the first word I learned to spell when I was six years old because I'd heard her so much. A sack of groceries was in the back with a loaf of our favorite sourdough bread sticking out the top, scenting the car. Mama squeezed my arm, and I was careful not to show pain on my face.

"How is he?" she said.

"He wiggled his toes."

"That sounds good."

"It is."

"How's his head?"

I gave her a curious glance. "He doesn't have any head injuries."

"I'm talking about his spirits. Baby, you don't get run down by a white gang and not have it affect your state of mind somehow."

I stared at the windshield and tried to arrange my face. "What makes you think he was run down by a white gang?"

"Because I am not stupid," she said.

She shot me a don't-you-try-to-pull-anything-with-me-girl look. I could feel it on the side of my face.

"Denny's?" I said.

"We need Sizzler tonight," she said. "Your celebration got interrupted last night. We got to make up."

"That's cool," I said.

I didn't see it coming: the nice steak and the gooey dessert leading up to the lecture. It had been so long since I'd had one, she was halfway into it before I realized what she was doing.

"Everywhere you go, certain people are going to try to stir you up," she said.

"Uh-huh."

"You just have to ignore them, Brianna."

"I try."

"Well, Ira didn't."

I stopped poking a strawberry on my shortcake and looked at her.

"He didn't ignore them," she said. "He walked right into their game. "

"He's paying for it now, Mama. I don't think he'll do that again."

"I'm not talking about Ira."

"You're talking about me."

"Mmm-hmm."

I put down my fork and rolled my eyes.

"Don't you be doing that, girl-child, or so help me I'll roll your head."

She hated it when I rolled my eyes worse than anything, but it was worth it if I could make her believe this was all just an annoyance for me.

"Mama, it's handled," I said.

"What do you mean, 'It's handled'?"

"Just don't worry about it."

She slammed down her water glass, sloshing its contents all over her hand. "Your boyfriend is lying there half-alive in a hospital bed because of some white racists, and I'm not supposed to worry about you?"

I kept my face stiff. "Why would you?"

"Because I know you. You can't keep your mouth shut; now you know that."

"Thank you, Mama. I really appreciate your confidence."

"Confidence has got nothing to do with it. I know how you feel about Ira. All somebody has to do is say the wrong thing, and you're going to be all over them. Then you'll be getting hurt; that's all I'm saying."

"You don't think I know that by now? I wasn't sleepwalking through that park when Prentice—"

"Brianna, just listen to me. If there is trouble, you walk away from it, and you come right to me."

"And then what?" I said. It came out sharper than I meant it to, but at this point it didn't really matter. I knew what was coming.

"Then we decide if this is a safe place for us."

"You're blowing this way out of proportion!" I said.

"I'm a mother. That's my job." She reached over and took my hand, but I didn't squeeze back. My insides were doing enough squeezing.

"I'm just being cautious," she said.

"You're just being paranoid."

"Don't get smart with me now. I'm saying what I think is right."

"Okay, you said it. Thank you."

"Excuse me?"

I looked up at her. Her eyes were hurt.

"I'm sorry," I said sullenly. "I just don't need all these warnings. I know you're trying to protect me—"

"Then let's drop it," she said.

We did. We dropped it into a prickly silence.

I rode home with her, painting a picture of loneliness in my head.

CHAPTER NINE

I WAS IN BED FOR EIGHT HOURS THAT NIGHT, BUT I didn't sleep any more than I had the night before. I'd flop to one side and see Ira lying flat on his back, trying to sleep through pain. I'd flop to the other side and see my mother looking at me all hurt and making her plans to move us at the next sign of trouble. Then I'd flop back, and the Flagpole Girls were holding their balloons and saying all the wrong things.

I didn't get to sleep until about two, and then only because I kept hearing Cheyenne saying, "I'll tell God that next time we talk."

They had prayed. But I'd tossed it off as a feeble response.

I'd prayed myself—and had put about as much faith in it as I did in Mrs. Quao pulling me into the bosom of her family. What had I come out with but a portrait of my own confusion and bitterness?

"I'll tell God that next time we talk," Cheyenne had said.

I bet she did talk to God. Cheyenne could talk to anybody, whether they really wanted to hear her or not. She probably told *Him* how many more days till spring break.

I'd always thought of it more like connecting to God. That was the way I prayed, not in words.

But no connecting was going on right now. That pretty much completed the loneliness, and I couldn't stand that.

Talk to God for me, Cheyenne, I thought at about 1:55. The next time I looked at the clock, it was six. Mama was in the shower, and a note was on the table. *You'll need to take the bus today. I have to go in early.*

So I wasn't in the best mood in first period. Mama was mad at me. I missed Ira. I missed God. I wanted to pinch somebody's nose off. Mr. Lowe stepped right into my trap.

"Brianna, may I see you out in the hall?" he said about halfway through class.

I looked up from the copy of *Hamlet* I wasn't reading to find him standing over my desk. He had a bald head that was so shiny the fluorescent lights reflected off it. He squinted at me through his glasses, and I just wanted to cartoon him the meanest way I could.

"Am I in some kind of trouble?" I said.

He looked surprised. "No, not at all. I just want to talk to you."

I gave a big ol' sigh, rolled my eyes, and threw my shoulders back so I could walk all bad down the aisle. I should have saved myself the trouble. Nobody even looked up from Act II, scene ii.

Out in the hall, Mr. Lowe closed the door behind us and looked at me over the top of his glasses this time. I folded my arms and waited.

"I'm curious, Brianna," he said. "Why would you think you were in trouble?"

"That's about the only time my teachers talk to me," I said. I didn't know where that came from. It was just part of nose-pinching.

"I apologize then," he said. "I certainly never intended for you to feel neglected. You and Seymour—Ira—just seem to want to keep to yourselves."

He looked like he didn't know where to go from there. He took off his glasses and started to clean them on his Mr. Rogers sweater. I didn't feel so tough.

"Don't worry about it," I said, as if he had brought it up. "I'm about used to it."

"Well, you shouldn't have to be. I'll try to rectify the situation in my class."

"It's all right," I said. I was wishing I hadn't said anything.

"No, it isn't all right. I'm a teacher. It's my job to meet the needs of each of my students."

His face was turning red, and on the word "students" he even spit a little. I pretended not to notice.

"Thank you," I said.

"I didn't bring you out here to discuss that," he said. "But I'm glad you said something. I certainly am."

He always talked like a book you would read in his class. That was all I'd ever really noticed about him. But now, I saw that he was flustered. It was the first real emotion I'd ever seen him display. It was making me uncomfortable.

"What did you want to talk about?" I said.

"Well, Ira, actually," he said. "How is he?"

It was my turn to look surprised. "He's messed up pretty bad," I said. "But they did surgery, and with therapy he should be all right. He can wiggle his toes."

I was sick of saying that to people, but it was the only real sign I had that Ira wasn't going to spend the rest of his life in bed. It seemed good enough for Mr. Lowe.

"That's a relief," he said. "I don't want to rush things, but when do you think he'll be ready for some homework?"

I wanted to say Hamlet and Gertrude were about the last things on Ira's mind and Mr. Lowe was pretty much of an idiot to even mention it, but I chewed on my lip to make him think I was considering it.

"Not anytime soon," I said. "He's still on a lot of pain medicine."

Mr. Lowe nodded thoughtfully and cleaned his glasses again. "You let me know when he's ready then," he said. "I'd like to see you tutoring him."

I laughed before the phrase was even out of his mouth. "You want *me* to tutor him?"

"Is that funny?"

"It is to me. In case you haven't checked it out, Mr. Lowe, I'm not Elizabeth Barrett Browning or somebody."

"Nor do you need to be. I just think you'd be the perfect one to bring Ira back up to speed when the time comes."

"Whatever," I said.

"I'll take that as a yes," he said. "You say the word, and we'll set you up."

I must have given him a weird look because he squinted his eyes at me again. "You have a good mind," he said. "I don't know that you always use it, but I've seen the glimmers of intelligence."

"Mmm," I said, abruptly.

"I don't know what 'mmm' means," he said.

"I don't think you want to know."

"Yes, I do. I surely do."

I rubbed the back of my neck with both hands. "I don't mean to be rude, but I haven't seen anything in this class I *wanted* to use my mind for. What does some prince going on for four hours about whether or not to kill his bad self have to do with what I've got going on? Some Shakespeare dude is going to show me what to do when most of the students in this school don't even acknowledge my existence and some of the rest of them don't think I *should* exist and they're out there trying to kill my man and telling me to make myself invisible . . ."

I stopped my mouth and pressed my lips together hard. Mr. Lowe slowly put his hand up to his own mouth and massaged his face with his fingers. His eyes were down to scared little cracks behind his glasses.

"It's been a long time for me, Brianna," he said.

What he was talking about, I didn't know, and I didn't care. I was making a fool of myself, and I wanted out of there.

"Are we through?" I said.

"Of course. Do you need to go somewhere, get yourself together?"

"No," I said.

He nodded, but he went back into the classroom and left me out there. I had the feeling I could have stayed in the hall the rest of the period, and it would have been all right with him. I was too shaken up to wonder why.

But I had about ten minutes to think about that. The moment I came out of first period, I had Eden, Laraine, James, and Harlan on me. I don't think my feet touched the floor all the way to my locker, they were walking that close to me.

"How's Ira?" James said. Poor thing had about the homeliest face I had ever seen on a brother—he had a small face, but all his features were big, which gave him a crowded look. He wore dreadlocks, which normally are cool, but on him, no.

But right then I didn't feel like being sorry about James's bad genes. I flung open my locker, and I didn't even look at him when I talked to him. "You must be all kinds of upset about him. You haven't even been to see him."

"We haven't been *nowhere!*" Eden said. She had blue eyes and creamy skin from her white mama, and her smooth bob was about the color of hot chocolate. She was pretty, except for the cowering way she carried herself. She was bent over like a question mark that day.

"Why not?" I said.

"I'm scared to go out! All of us are."

Tall, lanky-armed Laraine nodded the cornrows.

"What are you talking about?" I said.

They looked at Harlan. Of the four of them, he was the one Ira always said could make something of himself if he would quit being such a wimp and tomming with white people. He was in band. I'd heard him play the saxophone, and girl, he could wail that thing. He cut up something wild when he was with us and with people he was 100 percent sure accepted him. He would about do anything to get a pat on the head. But make him think he wasn't getting it, and he would disappear right into the wallpaper.

He looked miserably at me, his face all hanging.

"What?" I said. "I don't have time to play *Jeopardy* with y'all, okay? I got to get to class."

"They been harassing us," he said.

"Who?"

"Van Hessler."

"And that other dude," Eden said. "That Garrick boy. He followed me all the way into the building this morning, pinching at me."

Laraine started to cry right there. James looked at her, looked at Harlan, looked at me.

"I know it," I said to them. I stuffed my government book in my backpack.

"So?" Eden said.

"So what?"

"What do we do?"

I slung my backpack on my back and looked at them. They were all watching me, the way I'd probably watched Ira yesterday. I was pretty sure I felt the same way he had. *I can't fix this!* I wanted to shout at them. *You're on your own—all of you!*

But that would have been like putting the Little League in Candlestick Park. They wouldn't even know where to start.

"All right, look," I said. "Ira says he's going to get us some help."

"What kind of help?" Eden said.

"I don't know. Why don't you visit him in the hospital and ask him instead of hiding in your house like some kind of hostage."

"We *are* hostages!" Laraine said.

"Oh, you are not either. Get a hold of yourselves, all of you. Now."

They stared at the floor in agony. I pushed through them and turned to look at their defeated backs.

"One thing you can't do is walk around here all looking like you got something to be ashamed of. Put your heads up; don't you go shuffling."

They turned to me. James's features were scrunched together.

"So what are you saying?" Harlan said.

"I'm saying walk proud and stay out of their way until I find out what kind of help Ira has for us," I said.

"Is that what you're doing?" Eden said.

"Yes," I said.

I hadn't known it until right then, but it sounded good. Better than anything else I'd come up with anyway. I nodded firmly. "Go on to class now," I said.

They didn't, so I turned and went myself. When I glanced over my shoulder, they were all looking at each other and nodding. Mmm-*mmm*.

We had a sub in government. While everybody else was passing notes and telling jokes at the pencil sharpener, I doodled in my notebook. If Ira had been there, we would be playing tic-tac-toe and seeing what my name looked like attached to his. *Brianna Quao. Mrs. Brianna Quao. Mrs. Ira Quao.*

I carved it angrily into the page. Ira *wasn't* here, and I was feeling a burden of responsibility I could barely lift, much less carry on my shoulders. I drew a giant backpack with James, Harlan, Eden, and Laraine's heads sticking out of it. When the sub walked past, I balled it up and threw it away.

I could draw in government, but I sure didn't have it in art class. I got the girl next to me to explain what we were supposed to be doing, but I still could only stare at the blank piece of paper. Experimenting with shadow—that had as much to do with my life as *Hamlet*.

I used a sketchpad for backing, took the paper to the corner, and sat on the floor. A thin light shafted in through the window above me, and I was close to the speaker so the music muffled most of the talking into a background blur. But it still wouldn't come. When Ms. Squires's shadow fell across the page, it was the only one there.

"Yesterday was your day off," she said. "I didn't give you a week's vacation."

I looked up for the square gleam in her eyes. There wasn't one.

"I know," I said.

"Then why aren't you working?"

I shrugged.

She squatted down beside me. "You're not giving me attitude, are you, Brianna?" There was a warning in her voice.

"No," I said.

I started to rub the side of my pencil lead across the paper, but she grabbed my hand. "Look at me," she said.

I looked straight ahead.

"Where's all this coming from?" she said.

"All what?" I said.

"All this I-can't-work-today. Art is a discipline, Brianna. You might not have the inspiration every day, but you can't just sit there and wait for the spirit to move you."

She was about hemorrhaging sarcasm. I wanted to come right back on her. I wanted to say I wished the spirit would move *her* right back across the room. But I just pulled my hand away and said, "All right. I'll draw."

She gave me a long look and opened her mouth to say something. I stared at my page and got my pencil going. She stood up and went away.

Shadows? She wanted shadows? She didn't even know what shadows were.

Bearing the pencil down hard on the paper, I formed the darkest shapes of evil I could come up with. Then I made the lightest. I made them all converge on a hunched-over girl in a corner with a cap of kinky hair. And I made her as black as I could make her.

I flung it on Ms. Squires's desk when the bell rang, and I left.

CHAPTER TEN

TOBEY MET ME AT MY LOCKER AFTER SCHOOL, CAR keys in hand. "You ready?" she said.

I blinked at her.

"To go to the hospital," she said. "I told you I'd take you from now on."

I concentrated on loading up my backpack with homework I knew I wasn't going to do. "You don't have to," I said.

"I know. I want to."

"I feel like I'm putting you out," I said.

"The heck with how you feel. *I'm* feeling helpless, and I want to do something."

I looked up to see her eyes dancing like a pair of sparklers. I let myself grin. "As long as it's about you and not me," I said. "You got that heater working?"

"It's iffy," she said. "But it's not as cold in there as Cheyenne wants you to believe. She likes to be the martyr."

"That's one thing I *don't* want to be, girl," I said. I hoisted my pack up onto my shoulder and followed her toward the parking lot.

She was quiet until we had climbed in her car and she had started the motor. Then she said, "Do you feel like a martyr sometimes?"

"You mean like Joan of Arc or something?"

She shook her head and deliberately didn't look at me as she glanced over her shoulder to back out. "No. I was thinking more like Martin Luther King, Sojourner Truth, somebody like that."

I rolled my eyes out the window. Tobey would have been the last one I'd have figured for the liberal white trying to show the poor black that she was hip to her history. I hoped she would drop it because I didn't want to get into an argument.

She quieted down until we were turned onto MaeAnne.

"It has to be hard," she said.

"What?" I said.

"Being black."

"Only as hard as whites make it."

I wanted to bite my tongue right off as soon as I said it. I could hear Mama now saying, "Brianna, girl, I told you, you just don't know when to keep your mouth shut."

Tobey gripped the steering wheel and paid a little too much attention to the passing traffic. I folded my arms.

"I didn't mean you personally," I said.

"Oh, I know," she said.

I didn't believe her, but that was too bad. I couldn't worry about this right now.

"So what do we do?" she said.

"About what?"

"About making it easier to be black."

"Like I said, I wasn't talking about you personally," I said. *Let it be, Tobey.*

"You would tell me if I offended you or your race though, wouldn't you?" she said.

"Sure," I said.

We fell silent again. I hated it. What was going on? I mean, Tobey and I had been through some *stuff* together. The two of us had taken care of Cheyenne when she was going through her thing right after Christmas, and Ira and I had been there for Tobey when all that mess was happening with Coach Mayno in September. How come now, when I needed her, she—

No, it was me who wouldn't let her help.

Because she couldn't. It was that simple. She could ask me all the questions she wanted about being a martyr and about Martin Luther King or Malcolm X or whomever, but it was all words.

"I'm praying for you all the time," she said. "You and Ira."

"Thanks," I said.

"But I think Ms. Race is wrong. I think we could be doing a whole lot more."

"You don't need to be worrying about it," I said. "Ira's going to get us the help we need."

"Really?" Tobey pulled up to the stoplight at the corner across from the hospital and looked at me. "From whom?"

"I don't know," I said. "Ira just says he's going to get us help."

"Cool," she said. But she sounded about as excited as a pile of mashed potatoes.

"You don't think he can do it?" I said.

"I'm sure he can. I was just thinking, I wish it was us."

She shrugged and put the car in gear. I looked back out the side window, and my mouth came open. "Oh no," I said.

"What?"

I didn't have a chance to say it. Before I could get out the words, the figure I'd spotted on the corner had hurled something at Tobey's car. An entire red Slurpee smashed its icy self across the windshield.

Behind us, horns gave annoyed honks, and Tobey started to edge the car forward.

"No, girl, you can't see where you're going!" I said. "Turn on your wipers."

She flicked on the windshield wipers, and they shoved the ice to the side, leaving a red smear so thick I could have taken a chisel to it.

"You have a towel in here or something?" I said.

"Uh, yeah. Under the seat."

Her voice was shaky. I knew what her insides must feel

like. Cute white girls who lived in the Foothills didn't have fast food thrown at their vehicles. I got out to the tune of blasting horns and pushed the towel across the sticky ice. The guy behind us revved his motor and careened his Mustang around us. He gave me a long, ugly stare as he shot out into the traffic. I just kept wiping.

"You want me to help?" Tobey said out her window.

"I got it," I said. "What do you want me to do with this towel?"

"I don't . . . just throw it in the backseat . . . don't know."

I got in the car and stuck the towel between my feet on the floor. "You better get moving, or we're going to have some road rage happening here," I said. "Just pull up front and drop me off."

"I was going to come in and see Ira, but—"

"Don't even think about it, girl," I said. She was totally disoriented. I didn't think she would make it to any place but the safety of her own house.

She steered the car up to the front and shoved it into park. Even her lips were white.

"Was that one of those boys? Van or one of them?"

"Garrick," I said. "He's just a fool. Don't worry about him."

She leaned back in the seat and tried to giggle. "That was it? That was the 'danger' Ms. Race is worried about? A cherry Slurpee?"

"I think it was strawberry," I said.

"I'm bummed," she said. "I expected at least a semi-automatic weapon. I mean, come on."

She was trying to joke, and I was trying to act like I believed her. But we were both shaken half out of our jeans.

"You okay, girl?" I said.

"Oh, yeah, I'm okay. How about you?"

"I'm about to chew nails, but I'm fine," I said. "You better get to a car wash before that stuff starts eating your paint job off."

"It's not like anybody would notice if it did," she said. Her voice was sounding more even, but she was still clinging to the steering wheel. "What time you want me to come back to pick you up?"

"Mama's coming for me," I lied. Actually, Mama was going straight home to get ready to go to her singles group at church that night. But I wasn't about to drag Tobey back here. About now, all I could hope for was that she got home before it really hit her that she had just been violated and started to freak out.

"Okay then," she said. "If you're sure you're all right."

"It's going to take a lot more than this to get to me," I said. "They would call this pitiful in Oakland."

"Sounds like a great place," she said.

I waited until she drove off to go inside, just to be sure Garrick didn't jump out of the bushes with a cappuccino or something. Then I hurried through the lobby to get to the already jammed elevator before it closed.

I lied to Tobey, I thought as I squeezed myself in. *I'm every bit as scared as she is. I feel like I've just been slapped in the face.*

There was something about the disrespect in what Garrick just did, the total lack of regard for our dignity or Tobey's property. Those guys just thought they could do whatever they wanted and get away with it.

I was thinking so hard, I barely noticed that the woman next to me was pressing herself closer to the person on the other side of her so she wouldn't have to touch me. I didn't notice the tall dude in the back until I was almost to Ira's floor and just about everybody else had gotten off. One look, though, and I turned my head right sharp away.

It was Van Hessler.

Be cool, girl, I told myself. *What's he going to do in an elevator with other people around? Just don't look at him. Just get off on the fifth floor and don't look at him.*

But he was looking at me, no doubt about that. I could feel his eyes poking into my back, the way he would have gouged me with a stick if he had one. As it was, the minute the doors opened to the fifth floor and I made my move, I felt something sting me, right in the backside. Like fingers pinching me.

It was all I could do not to turn around and slap his face.

Make him invisible, I thought. *You can do it, girl. Just keep on walking like he's not even there.*

I had the tremors bad by the time I reached Ira's room though. I had to take three deep breaths before I went in, just so he wouldn't see that I was, as Cheyenne would say, "about to hurl."

Ira himself looked a whole lot worse than I felt. He looked like he was ready to jump out of casts, skin, and nerve sheaths. His face was twitching, and his eyes were all over the place. It didn't take a brain surgeon to figure out what was wrong.

I didn't even waste time saying hello.

"Was Van in here?" I said.

His eyes gave him away. He couldn't even keep them still long enough to look at me.

"What did he say?"

"He was just shooting off his mouth. Nothing new."

"What did he say, Ira?"

"You don't need to know."

I slapped my hands against his bed bar. "That's what got you into this mess in the first place, boy. Your not telling me what was going on! Now come on! What did he say?"

"There's a piece of paper in the drawer in the table," he said.

"What?" I said.

"Just get it."

I pulled open the drawer in the nightstand and pulled out a folded piece of binder paper. A phone number was on it, written in a woman's handwriting.

"What's this?" I said.

"That's your help."

"Who is it?"

"Just call it. And make sure your mama isn't listening."

"But who is it?"

"Just call it!"

"Ira, I am not going to dial a number and get somebody on the phone when I don't even know who I'm calling. Why won't you tell me?"

"Because we have to do it this way!"

His voice was so thick, I knew he was about to cry. I looked at the number again. "Who wrote this?"

"The nurse. I asked her to. And don't go asking her because she doesn't know. Come on, baby, I'm getting scared."

"Okay," I said. His words were teetering on the edge, and it was scaring me, too. I stroked his cheek with my finger. "I'll call tonight. Mama's going out."

He closed his eyes. "It will be all right, baby. Just trust me. I won't mess it up again."

Then he fell asleep.

I was a pincushion all the way home on the bus. Every thought I had was poking me.

Mama noticed it, I know she did, but she didn't say much to me through supper except to ask me how Ira was and to tell me she saw my show that morning.

"You were at school?" I said. "Why didn't you find me?"

"I didn't think you wanted to be found," she said.

"Mama, I'm not mad at you."

"You're mad at somebody."

I looked at her over a forkful of baked potato.

"Your paintings are beautiful," she said. "But, baby, they are angry."

I didn't say anything.

"Don't let it destroy you," she said. "That's all I ask."

Her words were like another pin sticking in me. Was there anybody *else* who wanted to poke one in?

I was doing the dishes when she left. As soon as she was

gone and I'd locked all three of the locks on the door, I plopped myself down in the beanbag chair and pulled the phone number out of my jeans pocket.

Several times in my life things happened that didn't seem real to me. It was like the difference between a realistic painting, in which the artist creates a photographic memory, and a surreal painting. You've seen those Dali works where a pocket watch melts over the edge of a table? That's what I mean.

When we got the phone call about Prentice and I went down to the park to find him lying under the basketball hoop with the life running out of him, that wasn't real. I was moving in slow motion. The world was like a smear around me, all thick and blurred. Maybe that was the only way I got through it, just thinking of it as a painting that wasn't real.

But it wasn't art. It was real.

As some-other-world as I felt right now, this was real, too. I had a piece of paper in my hand, and the very feel of it was dangerous. But if I didn't use it, maybe even worse things were going to happen. And I couldn't take any more of that.

Still, as I went to the kitchen and picked up the phone, something very real rushed through my head. It was like a film on fast forward of Tobey, Norie, Cheyenne, Shannon, and Marissa. I looked at the number again. I sure wished I was calling the Flagpole Girls, telling them to get on over here so we could pray and put together a Plan of Action that would make me feel safe, and give me hope just the way we had done for Tobey, Norie, and Cheyenne.

But Ms. Race, much as I resented her, was right. This was way more than a group of white girls could handle.

"*I'll tell God that the next time we talk,*" I could hear Cheyenne saying.

"God," I said aloud, "I sure wish I could talk to You."

The phone rang in my hand, and I startled right up against the wall. It had to ring a second time before I could get my breath to answer it.

"Hello?" I said.

"Dillon Wassen could die," said a girl.

"Who is this?" I said.

The voice grated on the edge of my familiar zone, but I couldn't place it.

"Don't matter," she said. "What matters is, if he dies, a Slurpee on your windshield isn't gonna be the half of it."

CHAPTER ELEVEN

"WHO IS THIS?" I SAID.

But she hung up, loudly, in my ear. I didn't even put down the phone. Instead, I clicked the hook, punched in the numbers on the paper, and hoped they were the right ones. My hand was shaking so hard I could barely see what was on the sheet.

The dude who answered obviously was a brother. I don't know how you can tell; you just can. But he had to say "Hello" twice before I could answer. What do you say when you don't even know who you're calling?

"Ira told me to phone you," I said.

"Brianna Estes," he said.

"Yeah!"

I was about to melt on the floor. A connection.

"You ready?" he said.

"For what?"

"Be at the Box on McCarran and MaeAnne at lunch tomorrow. Bring all the brothers and sisters you can find. I'll meet you."

"But I don't even know who you are!"

"I'll give you the sign, girlfriend."

"What sign?"

I got another click in my ear. I stood there staring at the receiver.

By the time Mama came home, I was twisted every which way but right side out, and the last thing I wanted was for her to see it. Thank the good Lord she didn't seem to be seeing much of anything. She was all preoccupied with whatever went down at the singles group and whatever was going through her mind as she spread out her clothes for the next day and sat down at the dinette table to do the bills.

I was glad she wasn't asking me any questions, but she was one more knot in my insides. The lines were getting deeper in her face, and tonight her eyes looked sunken.

I sniffed to myself. I wondered if Tobey or Shannon or any of them worried about their mama as much as I did over mine. Probably none of them had to.

The next morning I jumped every time Mama scraped a chair or banged a pot. I'd have sworn I was wearing every one of my nerves on the outside.

"You want me to drive you to school, baby?" she said.

"No!" I said.

"Fine." She pressed her lips together and turned away from me.

"I didn't mean it like that," I said. "You just have so much on your mind you don't need to be worrying about driving me. I'll take the bus."

"Suit yourself," she said.

Mmm-mmm, it was *cold* in that apartment. I went down to the bus stop early just to get away. I was going to have to fix it with her once this was all over.

And I had a strong feeling today was going to be some kind of turning point in making sure it was going to be over. I still had no idea who I'd been talking to on that phone, but his voice was surer than anybody's I'd heard since this whole thing started. Sure was all I wanted.

I pulled my faux-leather jacket tighter around myself and looked down the street for the bus. There was only a Jeep coming, with Norie at the wheel.

She pulled over to the curb and leaned across to open the passenger door. Her windows zipped, so she about never opened them.

"Get in," she said. "We're going to be late."

"What?"

"I'm your limo. Get in before the bus plows into me."

I scooted into the seat, pulled the door shut, and she took off. Norie drove like she did everything else—full out.

"What are you doing over here at this hour?" I said.

"Picking you up. I'm glad you were out there. I wasn't sure which apartment was yours."

I shook my head.

"There was no way I was letting you take the bus," she said. "Tobey told me what happened at the hospital yesterday with that guy throwing a Slurpee on her car. Jackal."

"Is she okay?"

"Who, Tobey? Yeah, she laughed it off like it was no big deal, but you and I both know that's only the beginning."

I watched her closely. She wasn't talking a line to me. She knew what she was saying, and she meant it.

"Don't be telling her that," I said.

"Nah. Let her keep her innocence awhile, right?"

I had to laugh out loud.

"What?" she said.

"Like *you've* got all this street experience, girl," I said.

She grinned. Norie's grin was square, like the rest of her. It was a cool smile. I started to relax.

"I haven't exactly been in a gang fight," she said. "But I read."

I grunted.

"Go ahead and blow me off," she said, "but I educate myself to what's going on in the world the best I can. I'd hang out in dark alleys and get to know Crips and Bloods if my parents would let me. Honest."

I rolled my eyes at her. "You are a trip, girl," I said.

"Yeah, well, whatever. Okay, so what's going down now? Any more threats since yesterday?"

I only hesitated a minute before I told her about the girl who called me and about Mr. X.

"Didn't Hessler tell you to stay away from Jack-in-the-Box?" she said.

I nodded.

"But you're going anyway."

"Yes."

"Then I'm going with you."

I looked at her sideways. "I don't think you can pass."

"What, for African-American?" She did some kind of gangster-wannabe thing with her shoulders and then laughed. "So why would I have to 'pass'? Aren't you allowed to have white friends?"

I stared out the zippered window for a minute. It would be nice to have somebody I could halfway depend on there with me. I wasn't even sure Eden and the rest of them would show up. And if they did, what good were they going to do me holed up under the table?

"Okay," I said. "But if this Mr. X dude says you have to cut out, you do it. Those are my terms."

"You are so cool, Brianna," she said. She turned excitedly onto MaeAnne.

"This isn't some glamour gig," I said to her. "Nobody's going to call 'cut' so you can take a bathroom break."

"Uh, what was my first clue?" she said. "Some girl calls you up and says, if Dillon Wassen dies, you're dog meat, and I'm not going to take it seriously?"

I nodded. "I wish I knew how he was."

"Call the hospital. There's a pay phone in the theater lobby. You have change?"

Actually, I didn't. I'd used it all at the hospital the night of the accident.

"Here," she said. She dug into her real leather jacket and pulled out a handful of coins. "Take it all. You never know."

"I'll pay you back," I said.

"We're all paid for," Norie said. "That's the whole point of us being the Flagpole Girls."

For the first time I felt like real light was breaking through the cloud that was hanging over my head. It gave me the courage to run to the theater lobby and put thirty-five cents in the phone slot. And it made me start to pray.

Please, God, let Dillon be okay.

"Hello," I said when someone answered. "I'm calling to check on Dillon Wassen's condition."

"We don't give out specific information about patients," the woman said, as if she were holding her nose. "I can only give you 'good,' 'fair,' 'serious,' or 'critical.'"

"Give me that then please," I said.

There was a short pause. "Serious," she said.

I squeezed the receiver. "What does that mean?"

"I'm not at liberty to say. You would have to consult his doctor. Are you a family member?"

"No," I said.

"I'm sorry," she said.

I stood there deciding what to do next. She didn't hang up right away.

"I can tell you this," she said. "'Serious' is not always as bad as it sounds. If I told you 'critical,' that would be cause for alarm."

"Thank you," I said.

"You have a good day."

I at least had a better one than if she had said he was critical—or no longer occupying a bed. I tried to let that carry me through the morning. That and Cheyenne's coming to my locker to check on me—and to tell me I was going to feel a whole lot better once spring break got here. And Tobey handing me a note that said, *"I'm still praying. Your fellow Slurpee sufferer."* And Marissa and Shannon giving me a balloon that said, "You're Special." I felt kind of lame hauling that around, but it wouldn't fit in my locker, and besides, it was the thought. When third period came around I was even able to take the time to wonder if Ms. Squires was going to kick me out of the class. She didn't let me wonder too long.

"Brianna," she said, the second I walked in the art room. "Could you come into my office? I need to talk to you."

I saw my shadow drawing on her desk right off. I straightened my back for a showdown. I had to clear up this kind of mess so I could concentrate on lunchtime.

"Sit down if you want," she said.

She moved a stack of mats off a chair, and I sat. She perched herself on the edge of her desk because every other horizontal plane in the room was piled with art supplies. A big sign on her bulletin board said, "A clean desk is the sign of a sick mind."

"I owe you an apology," she said.

Of all the things that could have come out of her mouth, nothing could have made my eyes bug out more. I could feel them popping.

"I gave you a really bad time yesterday. I had no idea what had happened to your boyfriend."

I managed to get a shrug going. "How could you have known?" I said.

"True. I don't hang out in the faculty lounge. And you, of course, didn't *tell* me why you were skulking in corners and giving everybody the evil eye. You looked like you were planning a bomb threat."

"I do that when I'm upset," I said.

"Would you mind cluing me in next time? I hate it when I blunder like that."

I couldn't help staring at her. She had her arms crossed over her chest way high so that she was patting her own shoulders. She looked genuinely sorry.

I glanced at the desktop. "I'm sorry about the drawing," I said. "I'll do another one today."

She reached for the drawing and held it out at arm's length, the way middle-aged people do when their eyes start getting fuzzy. Mama did that sometimes.

"No, actually, you were on the right track," she said. "And

this technique we're working on right now, you've mastered it anyway. What I'm interested in is the content of this piece."

"That isn't a 'piece,'" I said. "It's just some old thing I scratched out because I was mad."

"Exactly. And it's powerful." She looked at me over my sketch, eyes narrowed. "Now don't go off on me; I'm going to tell you something you need to know."

I waited.

"Your work in the library is wonderful. I wouldn't have offered you the show if it weren't. But it's wonderful for a high school senior."

"I *am* a high school senior," I said.

She shook her head, making the pencil in her hair-knot rock precariously. "In age, maybe. But in here," She tapped her chest. "In here, you're far older, far more experienced maybe even than I am. You've lived, Brianna. I don't know what you've lived; I can just see it in your face." She tapped the drawing. "This is the first time I've really seen it in your work. How much do you know about African-American art?"

I shrugged. "Nothing."

"I think it's time then."

She put down the drawing, picked up a brochure, and held it out to me. "A show is opening at the gallery on California Street this Saturday, and I want you to go. In fact, I'm assigning it to you. It's free. Unless something dire happens in your schedule, you need to be there."

I ran my eyes down the glossy brochure in my hand. A modern, impressionistic painting was on the front with "*Salome,* Henry Ossawa Tanner" printed underneath.

"I want you to come back Monday with a paper telling me what grabbed you right in your soul," Ms. Squires said. She leaned toward me like she wanted to be sure I knew she wasn't playing with me. "You can't go unprepared. I want you to know what to expect." She nodded toward a rickety old student's desk by the door, which was about to fall apart under a stack of books. "See those?"

I nodded.

"You don't need to do what we're doing in class today. Find yourself a corner and look through those. They're all African-American artists."

"What am I looking for?"

"You won't know until you find it," she said.

The bell rang, and she swayed toward the door. I noticed that the Converse tennis shoes were red today. I gave her back the points I'd subtracted from her yesterday.

The books might have been interesting, if I hadn't been so keyed up about going to the Jack-in-the-Box in an hour and a half. I flipped through the pages and caught a few names. Edward Mitchell Bannister. He did some rustics. More Tanner—a lot of Bible stuff. Jacob Lawrence—a series of his panels was in there, chronicling the exodus of the southern blacks to the North in the first third of the century. I tried to concentrate, but his painting of a crowded waiting room made me think of the mob at the Box at lunch. His chaotic city streets made me think of Garrick throwing a Slurpee at Tobey's car. The abandoned shacks gave me an image of our apartment—empty as we were moving out. After that, I mostly stared at the pages and tried not to see anything.

When the bell rang signaling lunchtime, Norie didn't meet me at my locker. She was waiting outside the art room.

"I got out of journalism early," she said. "Let's go so we don't miss Mystery Man."

I'd questioned myself about letting her come several times during the morning, but now, with my knees knocking together the way they were and her all jazzed up, I was glad she was there. I hung on to the handle above the window in the Jeep all the way down MaeAnne and listened to her talk.

"I've been thinking about this," she said, "and I bet this is going to be some of Koretta's college friends, you know, from UNR. They have some honkin' big old basketball players over there, a lot of them African-American. I bet they would just love to scare the pants off these little jackals."

I just nodded. I was busy looking out the back window for Harlan's car. I'd told him between first and second periods that he needed to pull the others together and get them to the Box, but he hadn't looked too eager. Matter of fact, he had looked like, in his opinion, this whole thing was right up there with a mouthful of braces. It looked like he'd opted for the orthodontist, because I didn't see a sign of his Buick.

Which, it turned out, was because it was already parked in the lot at the Jack-in-the-Box when we pulled in. Norie pointed it out to me as she parked the Jeep.

"Isn't that Harlan's car?" she said.

"Yes. That's a miracle."

"Hey, if you told me to 'be there,' I'd do it. Not many of us mess with Brianna Estes when she has her mind set."

I couldn't help staring at her.

"Is that how I come off?" I said.

"Uh, yeah. You can be scary. Which isn't all that bad. It's like all that change I gave you; you never know when it might come in handy."

I sure didn't feel scary as we pushed through the glass doors into the crowd that was already forming. I felt as if I might step off a cliff any minute because I didn't know where it was. Norie pointed over to the corner.

"There's Harlan and those guys."

"Hiding," I said.

"They aren't the gutsiest people in the world, are they?"

That was an understatement. They were over there giving new meaning to the word "terrified." James was sitting in the center, eyes and mouth meeting at his nose, and Laraine was clinging to him like a piece of Velcro. What she thought he was going to do to protect her I don't know. His whole scalp was glistening with sweat.

Harlan was at least trying to act calm. He had his arm slung across the back of the booth, and he was gnawing on a toothpick. Anybody who didn't know him would have thought he was waiting for some chick to come by and pick him up. Eden was definitely not the chick. She was chewing a wad of gum like a cow doing cud and sweepin' that dining area with her eyes. When she saw me, she about vaulted the table.

"Chill," I said to her. "You got everybody in the place looking at you."

"They always look at us," Laraine said. Her lower lip came out. "I'm gettin' tired of people all pointin' and whisperin'. I almost didn't come."

"Right," Norie said.

I nudged her, and she zipped it up and sat down next to Eden, who looked at her suspiciously.

"Y'all know Norie," I said.

"Hey," Harlan said. "Wha'sup?"

Norie blinked. "Not much. You?"

He just nodded and worked his toothpick.

I shoved Laraine over and took the edge of the bench. I tried not to look like Eden did as my eyes swept the room.

"Who are we looking for?" Laraine whispered.

"I don't know," I said.

James's eyebrows went up.

"I thought you said Ira was sending us some help!" Harlan said. The facade slipped off his face like somebody's pants falling down.

"I did, and he is. I just don't know who it is."

"You are crazy, girlfriend!" Eden said. Her voice went up into falsetto. "For all we know, this could be some kind of trap!"

"Oh right," Norie said. "Ira's really going to lay a trap for you guys. Get a grip!"

They all glared at Norie. I kept my eyes on the front door.

"See anybody who looks promising?" Norie said.

I shook my head even as the door opened and a brother in a long trench coat stepped in. I'd never seen him before. That was a good clue.

"Maybe that's our man," I whispered to Norie.

But she didn't answer. She just shook her head and pressed her lips into a line.

"Why not?" I said. "Do you know him?"

"I know of him," she said. "And you don't want him to be your man."

I looked at the dude again. He had about six earrings in each ear and eyes like brass knuckles.

"Who is he?" I said.

"That's Crispus Weeks," she said. She looked at me soberly. "He's the leader of the Brothers of X."

CHAPTER TWELVE

"I'M TELLING YOU, BRIANNA," NORIE SAID, "HE'S BAD news."

I kept my eyes locked on Crispus as two more African-American boys joined him. They were much bigger, both of them, but they didn't have the chiseled look that Crispus had. You could tell he was the leader—the *mean* leader.

Norie was tugging on my arm. "Come on, you don't think this is what Ira wants, do you?"

I shook my head, but my wheels were spinning. *If this wasn't what he wanted, then why did he give me their phone number? And why hadn't he told me?*

It made me just mad enough to keep the shivers from creeping any farther up my spine. I stood up and waited for the dude to reach the table. He stopped about two inches from my face. His brothers stood on either side of our group like they were the Secret Service or something.

Crispus didn't say anything, and I wasn't about to be the one to start the conversation. He just looked into my eyes like he was trying to read me. Then he raised his hands in front of his chest, and holding them real close to his body, he crossed his two index fingers in an X. I stared at him stupidly.

"That's the sign for the Brothers of X," Norie whispered. "I'm getting you out of here."

She curled her fingers around my elbow, but Crispus

sizzled us both with a look that could have burned through chain. Even Norie stopped.

"She has to go," he said to me.

"She's all right," I said.

He shook his head and delivered a cutting glare to Norie's throat. She tightened her fingers on my arm.

Crispus didn't move much, but suddenly he was deep in Norie's space. Her face went white.

"We got to take care of business," he said. "And it ain't about you."

He put his hands on his hips, pulling his trench coat back slightly as he did. I saw the bulge in his pocket, and I turned halfway to Norie.

"Why don't you step off a little?" I said. "Just for a minute."

"I'm not leaving you," Norie said. She bored her little syringe-glare at Crispus—though she didn't leave it there long.

"I'll be fine," I said. "Let's not make trouble, okay?"

She didn't like it, but she nodded and backed off to the next table where she leaned against the edge and watched like a vulture.

Myself, I smiled slowly at Crispus. Anything to keep that hostility he carried like a weapon from blowing us all away.

"Thank you for coming," I said.

"A sister needs help, I'm there," he said.

"I appreciate it—I do—but you know, I don't think—"

Before I had a chance to go on, before I could tell him I'd rather he went back to Sutro where he belonged because I didn't want any more blood spurting out over this thing, one of his henchmen, the one with the ruby ring in his left nostril, gave a grunt. Evidently that spoke volumes because Crispus turned his head like it was on a switch and looked at the door. I could feel my brothers and sisters behind me wanting to crawl into the planter.

It was Van.

And not just Van, but that girl—that Rachel chick from my third-period art class with the black everything except skin. Another dude was with them, too. He was obviously older than high school, and I didn't know him, but he jarred something in me. I'd seen that pinched look on somebody's face before.

Van and Crispus gazed at each other across the room, and it was like an electrical current. People could feel it, I knew, from the way they stopped talking and stiffened in their seats. About the only sound was Laraine sniveling in the background.

"Is that the dude?" Crispus said to me.

I wanted to lie, but my face gave me away before I even opened my mouth. Crispus turned and looked with disgust at my group huddled at the table. He made a derisive sound between his teeth.

"You gonna stand behind this, or you gonna sit there like . . ."

I won't tell you what he called Harlan and James. The idea was, Crispus didn't think he had too much to work with.

He leaned on the table, and punctuating his sentences with back-alley vernacular, he did a slow burn at their frightened little knot.

"Long as you act like they more powerful than you, you gonna be lookin' behind you all your life. Now either get up off your tails and get it on, or just shuffle yourselves right on down the street."

Then he exploded off the table and went straight for the door. I swear, the tables moved to clear his path. By that time, Van, Rachel, and the other guy had disappeared from the doorway. I could see Van's tall form poised out in the parking lot.

Ring Nose looked at Harlan and James, who hadn't so much as blinked since Crispus had started in on them. He grunted and jerked his head toward the door. I started moving.

I took about half a step when Norie snatched at my sleeve. "What are you doing?" she said.

"I'm going out there," I said.

"Are you nuts? You're going to get yourself killed!"

Laraine bleated like a sheep, and Eden was hollering above the ominous hum of the kids in the Jack-in-the-Box, who were rushing to the windows to look out on the parking lot.

"I have to go," I said. "You don't leave a brother hanging."

"What is that, some kind of primeval code?"

I didn't know what she was talking about, and I didn't care. Crispus had already pushed his way out the door, and I shot off after him. I think I knocked over some girl's drink and stepped on somebody else's jacket, but I didn't hear their reactions. I did hear Norie, right behind me, saying, "Wait. I'm going with you."

I had to claw through a crowd of oglers at the door, who were pressing their faces against the glass and salivating to see a fight. By the time I got outside, Van and Crispus were already squaring off between two rows of cars. Their breath was hanging in the air between them like an atomic bomb cloud, but the explosion hadn't happened yet. They were still throwing foul language at each other, competing to see who could sound more like Satan himself. If I left out all the cuss words, there would barely be a sentence. As it was, they were interrupting each other so much, I could only catch snatches.

"—tried to kill him—" Van said.

"—he out there tryin' to save hisself," Crispus screamed back, "and that honky—off the mountain—"

"That's where he belongs—oughta be taken out—"

"Look to me like he done took *that* dude out—"

"He was fightin' for the cause. You want me to fight you? Keep standin' there—"

"I'll fight you. I'll kill you—come on—"

Norie was cutting off the circulation in my arm. "Bri-*anna!*" she said.

I got my mouth close to her ear and said, "If this breaks

loose, you get your white self out of here. They're not playin'."

"What are you doing?" Norie said.

I didn't answer. I wrenched away from her grip and yanked people aside by the sleeves of their flannels and jeans jackets as I headed for Crispus. The way I figured it, I had about ten more seconds to get between them and stop this, or it was going to bust open, and there would be no breaking it up without tear gas then.

Ring Nose grabbed for me, but I jumped out of his reach and flung myself in front of Crispus. His eyes registered about a second of surprise.

"Stop," I said.

"Move aside, sister."

"No. Now just hold on. Ira doesn't want this."

"Like I give a hang what 'Ira' wants," Van said.

The other white guy stepped up beside him and tightened his fists at his sides. "I don't think my brother cares what Ira wants either, witch!"

"You're Dillon's brother," I said.

"Yeah."

"How is he?"

Crispus grabbed my shoulder. "What you care how his brother is?"

"Because I want this all to be over!" I said.

"Oh, it ain't over," Van said. His lip curled. "Not until we seen the last of you . . ."

"Okay, okay," I said.

I turned to Crispus, whose nostrils were flared out to the sides of his face. His eyes glittered at me.

"You came here to help me, right?" I asked.

He gave a jerk of a nod and flashed his eyes back to Van.

"Okay," I said, "then all I want is to leave. And I won't come back. None of us will, okay?"

"No, man, you givin' in. That's chicken—"

I didn't give Crispus a chance to finish. I looked back at

Van. "Deal?" I said. "We don't come back to the Box. We stay out of your way. We pray for Dillon. You leave us alone."

Van's lip curled up into his nose. *"Pray?"* he said.

"That's right," I said.

"Ooh," Rachel said. It was the first thing out of her mouth, standing there next to Van, but she looked like a person who had been trying not to throw up and couldn't hold it back any longer. "Bring in the Gospel singers," she said. "Glory hallelujah, brother!"

I kept my eyes on Van. She wasn't even worth a look from me.

"Deal?" I said. "We leave; the Box is yours."

"That ain't no deal," Crispus said.

"Sure, we'll take it," Van said. He looked, poker-faced, at Crispus. "We'll stand here while you go."

Crispus took a step forward, but I put my hand on his chest. I could almost feel his nerves racing through his clothes.

"It isn't going to hurt anything for us to leave. It's no big deal," I said. "I don't want any more blood over this."

"Blood's the only way we gonna keep from bein' taken right on down back to slavery! We got to bleed—"

"Then bleed for somebody else," I said. "I don't need it."

With my hand still on Crispus's chest, I looked at Van one more time. He was standing there, cross-armed, with Rachel heaving her chest and the other guy, Dillon's brother, barely holding himself back. Only then, in the background, did I spot the black Cherokee with another short-haired dude at the wheel. It could only be Garrick, waiting for the getaway when the fight was over.

No big exit today, Garrick, I wanted to shout to him. *There isn't going to be a fight.*

"All right," I said to Van. "We're leaving."

"No, man," Crispus said.

"Come on, escort me to my car. I want protection."

It was the closest I could come to letting him save face. He bought it, halfheartedly. Crispus took my arm, and we turned away from Van. Ring Nose stepped in beside me, shoulder up to the top of my head. I could see a big *X* tattooed on the side of his neck. So much for Norie's idea about clean-cut basketball players.

I closed my eyes and prayed that nobody in the crowd would start clapping for the skinheads or make a comment to Crispus. If we could just get to the Jeep—

Behind us, I heard a vehicle screech to a halt. *Please don't let it be the police,* I thought.

"Hey," a voice cried out from that direction. I knew the voice. It was Garrick.

"Get back in the car, dude," Rachel said to him.

"What's goin' down?" he said.

"Unconditional surrender," Van said.

I felt Crispus tighten beside me. I tried to push on, but he was slowing down.

Just get to the Jeep, I prayed. *Please—*

From over the top of what I now knew must be the black Cherokee, came an empty laugh from the hollow soul of Garrick Byers. "That's it, be afraid, Ne-groes!" he shouted. "Be very afraid!"

That was it. It was over. Crispus unfolded like a switchblade and lashed at Van across the space that suddenly no longer existed between them. Ring Nose made a dive for Garrick, and Dillon's brother disappeared under Crispus's other bodyguard. All around us there was a roar, and legs, arms, fists were thrusting out and back like pistons gone wild.

"Stop it!" I screamed. "Stop!"

I felt a hard, sharp jab on my jaw, and the pavement came up and hit my cheek. Ice bit at the side of my face. Weight pressed on my back and then lifted, again, again, again, as people stepped on me in the fray that went on above me.

"Brianna!" somebody screamed.

I tried to reach up, but things were going black in front of my eyes. I couldn't see to get anything on my body going.

Then I was jerked up from under my armpits and dragged straight ahead through a leering mob of girls who all seemed to be shrieking things like "Get him! Pound that . . ."

I shut it out and forced my legs to move. Norie flung open the Jeep door and shoved me inside. I sat slumped in the passenger seat with my forehead on the narrow dash. She got in, pushed me back, and jolted the seat to a horizontal position.

The whole world reeled as she rammed the Jeep out of the parking place and squealed across the asphalt.

"I can't leave!" I said.

"We're doing it!"

"What about Eden? Laraine?"

"Dude, they ran the minute that Garrick kid started mouthing off. Do you need to go to the hospital?"

"No! No hospital."

I pressed my frozen fingers to the side of my face and looked at them. They were smeared with blood.

"I have a first-aid kit in the back," she said. "We'll see how bad it is, but if it's bad, I'm taking you—I don't care."

"You see Harlan's car anywhere? He's probably having heart failure."

"Uh, no," Norie said.

I squinted up at her. "What? What does that mean?"

She tightened her mouth. "I think Harlan took you down with his elbow when he was trying to get into the fight. He got right in there and started slugging it out beside Crispus."

"No way."

"Way." She shifted the gears and looked down at me. "They're going to follow the strongest leader, Brianna. And right now, Crispus is it."

CHAPTER THIRTEEN

NORRIE FOUND SOME BATHROOM AT SCHOOL I DIDN'T even know about, back in the shop section.

"You get around a lot when you're newspaper editor," she said. "Sit in that stall, and I'll wet some gauze and clean that out."

I sat on the edge of the open toilet seat, and that's when I started to shake.

Norie came in with the gauze and shoved my head down between my knees. "I'm not sure, but I think you're about to faint," she said. "Who can tell; you don't turn pale."

I snorted, and even that sounded shaky. I closed my eyes and felt the toilet going sideways.

"Whoa!" Norie said.

She grabbed me with both arms and held me against her. I could feel hot blood running to my head, and slowly the world turned right side up again. Norie pulled me up to face her.

"You look awful," she said.

"Bad hair day, girl," I said.

She grinned and gingerly touched my cheek with the gauze. I squeezed my eyes shut, but I held still.

"That was evil," she said.

"Uh-huh."

"That Crispus dude is going to get himself killed. Did you know that homicide is the leading cause of death for young black males?"

"Yes," I said. "That's how my brother died."

She stopped cleaning to look at me. "Your brother? When was this?"

"Four years ago."

"Somebody killed him?"

"Uh-huh."

"What? In a gang fight?"

I glared at her. "Prentice wasn't in a gang. He was ten years old. All he did was go down to a park to play basketball, and three white boys came along and didn't want him there. So they pulled out a gun and shot him."

She was staring at me, and I didn't blame her. Whenever I talked about Prentice—which wasn't often—I had to keep my face stiff, and my voice even as a line. Or I'd get hysterical. Koretta Quao had nothing on me.

Norie looked at me a minute longer, and then she studied my cheek again. Her lips were turning blue.

"How does it look?" I said.

"Not as bad as I thought. It's a scrape. You don't need stitches or anything."

"You know that from your daddy being a doctor?"

"He made me learn first aid, CPR, the whole bit." She sat down on the bathroom floor and tried to smile. "He didn't tell me it would make me feel like I was made of rubber though. Brianna, this is horrible."

"Tell me," I said.

I reached out and ran my hand real quick across the top of her head.

"You're not telling me anything when you say homicide's the leading cause of death among black boys," I said. "You tell me *why*, and you'll be telling me something."

She twitched her eyebrows. "Part of it's economics. African-Americans don't have anything close to equality with the average white American when it comes to money. The average wealth of black households is less than 10 percent of whites', which is, of course, because a black person has to be three times as good to get a job as an average white. You guys are worse off economically than you were in 1963. That could make a person mad enough to go out and get himself into situations where somebody's going to blow him away."

"Ira has money coming out his ears," I said. "Your daddy's a doctor. You know what they make. You live in the same neighborhood."

"Which is reason number two," she said. "Do you know what his family went through to get that house built and to move in? People over there at Caughlin Ranch were signing petitions to keep them out. You know, the old 'there goes the neighborhood' thing. Ignorance, that's what we're talking here."

I pulled away from the cream she was putting on my cheek. "You have any statistics on how we're supposed to stop *that?*"

She concentrated on screwing the cap back on the tube. "No," she said. "I don't think statistics can tell you that. I've been around and around about that with God."

I felt ashamed then. She packed up the first-aid kit, and I stared at the floor.

"How did you know all that, all those facts?" I said.

She snapped the box closed. "I've been doing a lot of reading, ever since the other day at the Box, the day Ira had his 'accident.' I thought, since civil rights, things were pretty much okay for blacks. Yeah, right." She stood up. "I know you don't think I can possibly understand because my skin is white and yours is black, but I think I get some of it, Brianna. Every time I read about how almost impossible it is for an African-American to get out of the mess we've made, I develop this lump in my throat. I haven't lived it, but I feel it."

I looked up at her.

"I just want to help," she said.

Slowly, I shook my head at her. "I don't know what you could do. I don't even know what to do. Crispus himself could be dead by now."

Norie squatted down again. "Look," she said. "From what I've read about the Brothers of X and seen on TV and all, they didn't lose that fight. It's probably over right now, and he and his big bookends—weren't those guys out of control?—probably kicked tail and took names, you know what I'm saying?"

I nodded.

"But the thing is, that isn't going to be the end of it."

"So much for us laying low and staying out of their way," I said.

"You're right in their spotlight."

"If you think you're helping me, girl, you're wrong. I'm getting *real* depressed."

"Well, the first thing you have to do, as I see it—I mean, if you want my advice . . ."

She waited, and I nodded.

"You have to see Ira this afternoon. I don't think he actually knows Crispus personally. He probably got the number from somebody else, but he needs to know what's going on. Maybe he could help call Crispus off. Not that he can do much from a hospital bed."

"He's done plenty already, as far as I can see," I said. "I am going to chew that boy's head off."

"Why don't you wait until he's out of traction," she said. "It'll be more fun that way." She stood up and stuck out her hand. I took it and let her pull me up. My legs were wobbly, but I was okay.

"I'll meet you after school and take you to the hospital," she said.

"Ms. Race wouldn't like this," I said. "Not that she cares, now that she's got herself a man."

"A man? That's a new one on me."

"Never mind," I said.

"I do kind of hate to do things behind her back," Norie said.

"I am *not* going to go to Mr. Holden, and that's what she would want me to do."

Norie put up both hands. "Okay, okay. No Ms. Race, no Mr. Holden. We'll do what we can. I'll pull up to the side door and meet you after sixth."

She didn't disappoint me. The Jeep was idling at the bottom of the stairs. I stepped right in. Wyatt was in the back seat—and Cheyenne. I shot Norie a look.

"We're going to need support," she said.

Wyatt raised his hand and grinned at me.

"And this is my day to tutor Cheyenne. We can work in the waiting room while you visit Ira."

"What happened to your face?" Cheyenne said. "Dude, that looks like it hurts."

"I fell in PE," I said.

"You did not either. You don't even take PE!" She scowled at me from under her dark bangs. "If I tried to lie to you, you—"

"All right," I said. I looked at Norie. "You didn't tell her."

"I wasn't sure if you wanted anybody to know. Although I did tell Wyatt."

"My lips are sealed," Wyatt said.

"Sealed about what?" Cheyenne said. "Would somebody tell me?"

So I filled her in. Her black eyes got as round as silver dollars, and her mouth fell open.

"You want me to take you home instead, Cheyenne?" Norie said, looking at her in the rearview mirror.

"No way! Brianna's in trouble, I'm there!"

"You just going to have to keep your mouth closed, though, girl," I said. "All I need is for you to tick off the wrong person."

"I do that, huh?" she said ruefully.

Wyatt gave an exaggerated nod, and she smacked him. I turned around and snuggled back into the seat. For the moment, I felt safe.

Until Norie pulled into the parking place out front, and we all saw them at the same time.

"Isn't that what's his name?" Cheyenne whispered.

"Van. Yeah," Norie said.

He was crouched on one knee in the grass out front, one arm around what looked like Rachel's shoulders and the other hand stuck out behind him, holding a cigarette.

"There's Garrick," Wyatt said.

"I don't see that other guy though. The big one he had with him this afternoon," Norie said.

"That was Dillon's brother," I said.

Norie looked alarmed. "You want to go in the back door?"

"I don't think he'll try anything with all of us around you," Wyatt said.

"Come on," Cheyenne said. "We'll protect you."

I smothered a laugh and got out. They would be about as much protection as a bikini in a thunderstorm, but at least they were more loyal than Eden, Laraine, James, and Harlan. My blood was still boiling over that.

So Wyatt walked on one side of me and Cheyenne on the other. Norie led the way, shoulders back, chin out. I stared straight ahead.

Still, when we passed them, I could feel the pointy looks, the curled lips, the faces all writhed up like they were enduring some horrendous odor. I could just *feel* it.

I waited for the shouted expletives, but there were none. They just stayed very still when we went by.

"That was eerie," I said when we got inside.

"Did you look at them?" Wyatt said.

I shook my head.

"Van has a black eye bigger than my fist."

"Garrick's lip was all swollen," Norie said. "You look pretty healthy compared to them. I have a theory."

"What?" Cheyenne said. She was talking at every possible moment. It was like letting steam out of a kettle for her.

"I think they got a taste of Crispus today, and they know they can't just throw their weight around," she said. "Who knows? Maybe it'll be enough."

Wyatt patted her arm. "Nice try, Nor,'" he said. "But I don't think guys with swastikas tattooed on their arms care too much about a little black eye."

"Swastikas!" Cheyenne said.

All three of us sprayed her with a *shh*.

Ira was awake and without one of his IVs. He was much calmer than yesterday, and he grinned when he saw his visitors.

"You look cute even with all those bandages and stuff," Cheyenne said. "You could be an advertisement for hospital beds or something."

"Bedpans," Wyatt said.

"How *do* you go to the bathroom?" Cheyenne said.

"Cheyenne, shut up," Norie said.

We all grinned, even Ira, and we talked about insignificant things, and then Norie announced it was time for her to tutor Cheyenne and Wyatt was going to help her. Cheyenne opened her mouth to protest, but they both grabbed an arm and dragged her out.

"I'm sure glad spring break is only a week away," she said as they went down the hall. "I'm sick of studying!"

"That girl is a trip," Ira said when they were gone. "Come here, baby. Just give me a kiss, would you?"

"No," I said. "Not after what you tried to pull on me."

His eyes clouded. "What?" he said. "What did I pull?"

"Crispus Weeks," I said. "Leader of the Brothers of X."

"You called," he said.

"I did."

"He wasn't supposed to tell you who he was."

"He didn't! He just told me to show up with Harlan and the rest of them at the Jack-in-the-Box—"

"No!"

"Well, yes. He came in there all ready to start a riot, which he did."

"No!"

"Why do you keep saying no, Ira? If you didn't want that to happen, why did you tell me to call him?"

"I didn't think he was going to drag you all into it. I thought he was going to take care of it on his own."

"Well, evidently that's not the way he operates. He likes to take everybody who's black down with him."

"Was there a fight?"

"You could say that. Look at this."

I pointed to my cheek. Ira's face folded, and I felt bad. I put my hand on his forehead.

"It's nothing, baby. I'm just mad, that's all. You know how I feel about violence, and you walked me right into it. I mean, even if you didn't know I was going to physically be there, I don't want any part of that mess. And now we're in it."

"How?"

"Harlan joined right in, and maybe James, too. Before you know it, they'll be piercing their noses and branding Xs on their behinds."

"Maybe Van will back off though."

"That's what Norie says. Wyatt says no."

Ira twitched an eyebrow, about the only thing he could actually move. "What do they know about it?"

"Well, more than most people, that's for sure. And they're all the help I have right now. So don't you go knocking it."

"Don't get all over me!"

"Why not? I have to get on top of this, Ira. I have to."

"Brianna."

It was a cold voice, coming from behind. I turned around to face Mrs. Quao.

She was all in black silk, like somebody died, and she had a turban around her head and hoop earrings. She was making some kind of statement before she even opened her mouth.

"Hi," I said.

"May I speak with you out in the hall?" she said.

I looked at Ira. He had his eyes closed.

"Sure," I said.

My heart started to pound. How much of that had she heard? All we needed was for her to get wind of this.

"I was just telling Ira—" I started to say.

To my surprise, she put a red-nailed hand on my shoulder. "I don't need to be privy to your private conversations," she said.

She let her hand slide off and folded it with her other one in front of her. Clinique filled my nostrils, and I stared at her glossy mouth. She was all gussied up for this occasion. It was almost like she had planned the scene.

"It's neither here nor there anyway," she said, "because there aren't going to be any more conversations with Ira."

"Excuse me?" I said.

"Saban and I have been talking, and although he isn't Ira's primary physician on the case, he *is* a doctor, and he feels that your visits upset Ira too much."

"I don't—"

"You don't have to understand, Brianna, honey, and I don't expect you to." She gave a smile that reminded me of clay. "I remember what young love was like. You think you have to spend every moment together. You think no one else can be as much for that person as you can. But in this case, that's nothing more than the selfish longings of puppy love."

What was she talking about? My heart had stopped pounding—stopped beating completely—and I know I was staring at her.

"So until Saban thinks Ira is more stable, we're going to ask you not to visit him anymore," Mrs. Quao said. "Are we clear?"

"No, we are not clear!" I said. "I don't understand this at all."

"I'm sorry."

She just kept standing there, kept smiling. I couldn't

move—until she reached out and patted my arm. Then I pulled away and bore my eyes into her hard. I even flashed a vision of Crispus stepping out of the shadow and taking her on.

I turned toward the door to Ira's room.

"Where are you going?" she said.

"I'm going to tell Ira what's going down."

"No. His father and I will handle that."

I ignored her and kept going, but her nails clamped around my arm and dug in ever so slightly. I stopped pulling. It was pointless.

"Go on home, Brianna, or I'll have to call a security guard," she said.

"I'm going," I said.

"If you really love Ira, you would want to do what was best for him," she said.

But I did love Ira, and I did know what was best for him, and this wasn't it. But telling her that would have been like slamming my head right against the wall. All I could do was turn around and go. I just wanted to get the smell of her perfume out of my nose, and the picture of her artificial smile out of my head.

I whipped past the waiting area and snapped, "Let's go!"

Norie, Wyatt, and Cheyenne scrambled up and chased after me. I didn't answer any of their questions until we reached the empty elevator.

"I'd like to go back there and tell her off!" Cheyenne said. "She has no right—"

"She has every right, Cheyenne," Wyatt said. "She's his mother."

"Mommie dearest," Norie muttered.

The elevator doors eased open, and I couldn't get out of there fast enough. I actually hoped Van and company would be there on the lawn and would say something to me. I was ready to spit, claw, and scratch the first person who gave me a reason.

And somebody did. I was the first one to see it as I stomped down the sidewalk. I stopped so abruptly, Cheyenne ran up the back of my leg.

"What?" she said.

I pointed. There was a unanimous gasp.

Norie's windshield was smashed, and the plastic zippered windows were slashed to ribbons.

CHAPTER FOURTEEN

I WANTED TO GO THROUGH THE CEMENT. JUST SINK down and pull it up over my head. First Tobey's car, now Norie's. Unlike Tobey, though, Norie didn't stand there and go into shock.

"Those jackals!" she said. "This is so evil!"

"Where are they?" Cheyenne said, looking around, fists doubled.

"Chill, Cheyenne," Wyatt said.

"Just let me at those jerks. I'm sick of this!" Cheyenne went on as if Wyatt hadn't said anything. "You can't just wipe this off like a Slurpee. What if one of us had been in there! You could lose an eye or something. You could bleed to death—"

"Cheyenne, shut up!" I said.

She looked at me like I'd slapped her. Those beautiful lips smacked together, and she tossed her head away from me. I wanted to kick myself right in the tail.

Norie squatted down to examine the shards on the sidewalk. "I told you, Brianna," she said. "This isn't over. We have to have a Plan of Action."

"No way," I said. "Ms. Race would never go for it."

"Fine," Norie said. "So we let Crispus Weeks handle it?"

We all fell silent. Wyatt cleared his throat and said, "Nor, you want to go call your mom?"

"Yeah, I don't know what else to do." Her eyes darted to

me. "She's going to insist on calling the police. You might not want to be around for that."

I nodded. "I can catch the bus. No biggie."

"You want me to go with you?" Wyatt said.

What I wanted was to be by myself. My head was about to spin right off.

The bus took its sweet time coming, which gave me a chance to think. Now the police were going to be involved. Ira had said they had been around once to cite him with reckless driving, but nobody had asked any penetrating questions. Without me there, they were unlikely to connect Norie's windshield with Ira's accident.

But that wasn't what really had me clinging to the back of the bus seat in front of me. It was two things that Norie had said.

This isn't over. We have to have a Plan of Action.

They're going to follow the strongest leader.

She was right. It was either going to be Crispus Weeks . . . or it was going to be me.

Mama was already home when I got there, and I could hear her slamming cabinet doors in the kitchen before I even opened the door. If I had had anyplace else to go, I wouldn't have walked in.

"Hey, Mama," I said.

"Come in here, girl-child," she said.

I dropped my stuff on the floor and ventured into the kitchen. She had her hair tied up on top of her head, and she was wearing her biggest, sloppiest sweats. The kitchen was sparkling—a sure sign she was working off something big.

"What's wrong?" I said.

"Well, now, what isn't?" she said.

I swallowed. "Did you have a bad day at work or something?"

"If that were the only problem I had, I'd be tap dancing in here."

"Oh."

"Yes, 'oh.' I got a good mind to start packing right now."

I started to shake.

"First I go to my group last night, and I look around at those people—and I can't even ask for prayer."

"Why not?"

"Because I'm sitting there thinking that every one of them is going to be thinking, 'If those kids can't keep themselves out of trouble, all the prayin' in the world isn't going to help.'"

"What?"

"That's the way I feel, Brianna. I can't even ask people to go to the Lord for this. Then I get this call from Koretta."

"Koretta?"

"Mmm-hmm. About five minutes ago. She called looking for you, all hysterical. I thought I'd do a good deed and try to calm her down so I asked her what was the matter, and she said she was worried about you."

Uh-oh. I couldn't stop myself. I put my hand up to my cheek.

"Is that what happened in the fight at the Jack-in-the-Box today?" she said.

I knew my eyes were bulging.

"Let me look at that," she said.

"It's fine."

"Get your hand down and let me see it." She gave my cheek a searing look. "What on earth were you doing in the middle of that?"

"How did Koretta know?"

"I have no idea. But don't you know she went straight to her mama and daddy—"

"Who came straight to me and told me I can't see Ira any more."

The deep lines on Mama's face smoothed out as her eyes drooped.

"Oh no, baby," she said. "Oh, I am so sorry."

I nodded. My throat was getting thick, and I wasn't about to try to talk past it.

"You want to know what I'm feeling?" she said.

I didn't, but I nodded.

"I feel like I just want to take you and run. Just fly right out of here and go—"

"Where? Where are we going to go where somebody doesn't hate us before we even open our mouths?"

"But you did have to open yours, didn't you?" she said. "How did that thing start at lunch today? I bet you were right there in it from the beginning."

"What was I supposed to do?"

"Walk away. That's what I've tried to teach you."

"I tried to!"

"Not hard enough evidently!"

"You don't know!"

She slammed her hand so hard on the counter the flour canister jittered.

"Don't you tell me I don't know, girl-child," she said. "I buried your daddy and your baby brother, both of them killed because they couldn't walk away."

"Prentice was playing basketball!"

"At a park I told him never to go to. I told him it wasn't safe for him down there."

"But he had every right to be there!"

"Rights don't mean anything to somebody who has hate in his heart. Your daddy should have taught you that."

"My daddy's death, you mean."

She looked at me. I looked back. We didn't have to say a thing. I knew we were both conjuring it up in our minds, the sight of my father twelve years ago, twenty-five years old, stepping into a fight between two kids on a street corner and being stabbed in the stomach by a boy his own color. It was an image I didn't paint in my head if I could help it. I didn't like the part in the corner, where my mother was screaming,

"See what happens? See what happens when you don't leave it alone!"

"We just came out of that cave, Brianna," Mama said now. The lines were back in her face, deeper and more tragic than ever. "If you are in trouble, we are not going to stay here and wait for it to happen to you, too."

"It's not going to."

"Can you give them what they want?"

"No," I said. "They want me to disappear. They don't want to have to look at any of us—Harlan or Eden—any of us. They have swastikas tattooed on their skin, Mama. I can't ignore that."

"Then there is nothing I can do but take care of my own," she said. "I'm going to take you to school in the mornings, and I want you to stay there until I can pick you up in the afternoons."

"What about the rest of the time?"

"We don't go out, period."

"Oh, Mama, come on!"

"Until this blows over. I can't take a chance with you, Brianna."

"I have to go to an art show tomorrow. It's an assignment for school."

"You're not going anywhere on that bus."

"Go with me."

"I can't. I promised to work for Habitat for Humanity tomorrow."

I threw myself out of the kitchen and marched to the couch where I flopped down and started to maul a pillow. She came in behind me and stood over me, arms crossed like she was afraid her heart was going to beat right out of her chest.

"All right," she said. "You take the car. I'll get a ride. But you may not go alone, you hear me? I want somebody with you at all times."

"Okay," I said.

"And if anyone lays a hand on you again, we are gone. We move on."

She glanced at her watch. "The meat loaf is almost done. You're not going out tonight."

"No, Mama," I said with a sigh. "I'll stay right here."

She licked her lips about twenty times, and then she disappeared into the kitchen. I put my head back on the couch and closed my eyes. I wished for that this-can't-be-real feeling, but it was all too true. The skinheads had made a prisoner out of me.

We need a Plan of Action, Norie had said.

I shook my head. There wasn't a thing I could do about this now. Not a thing except lay lower and lower. And lower.

After dinner, I sat by the phone and studied my Flagpole Girls list. If I had to take somebody with me to the art show, it had to be one of them. I was spitting mad at Harlan and the rest. Koretta was out of the question. Mama probably wouldn't hear of my asking anybody from the church.

Tobey and Norie were the logical choices, but I'd already gotten them into enough trouble. The way Norie's father was, he was probably cross-examining her about the broken windshield right this minute.

So I was left with Cheyenne, Marissa, and Shannon.

Cheyenne actually wasn't a bad idea. I felt like I owed her something, after the way I'd snapped at her on the sidewalk that afternoon. She was probably still pouting about that.

Somehow, I was drawn to Marissa on this, too. Twice she had squeezed my hand and tried to be on my side. I'd pretty much blown her off.

I thought you were planning a bomb threat, Ms. Squires had said.

Do I really come off that way?

I picked up the phone.

Cheyenne was about beside herself and ran off to ask Tassie, her foster mother, if she could go. Tassie would let her.

That woman thought all we Flagpole Girls walked on water after what we had done for Cheyenne.

Marissa sounded surprised, but she gave an immediate yes. "Shannon and I are still praying for you," she said before we hung up.

"Thanks," I said.

Shannon. I could hardly take two-thirds of the Shy, the Timid, and the Blabbermouth. I ought to invite her. Of course, on the other hand, she hadn't been all that support-ive. She seemed to be about the only one who sided with Ms. Race.

I dialed her number anyway, and she answered in her usual little mouse voice.

"Hey, girl," I said, with forced cheerfulness. "You want to go to an art show with me tomorrow?"

There was a short silence. "Sure," she said finally. "I've never been to one. That would be neat."

"I'll pick you up at one," I said.

"Um, I have to ask," she said.

She set down the phone with a thud, and I could hear her talking timidly in the background. I wasn't surprised, actually. As much of a scaredy-cat as she was, she probably didn't take a glass of water without asking permission.

What I didn't expect was the eruption that took place from across the room on her end. It was a deep male voice like the one I'd talked to on the phone that night, and al-though I couldn't hear what he was saying, clearly, he was about to have a hernia.

The phone picked up again, and Shannon said, "Um, Brianna?"

"Uh-huh."

"I—um—I can't go. Sorry. I didn't know we already had plans."

Plans. What, was somebody 'planning' to blow up? I could hear my voice hardening. "Don't worry about it," I said. "Have a good time."

I hung up before she could say good-bye.

So the skinheads weren't the only ones with racial hate running through their veins.

I dressed to the hilt the next day. An art show opening of an African-American exhibit was a good excuse to break out the kente cloth and make a wrap-top that I could wear under a flowing long blouse and with baggy chinos. I was a vision in green, khaki, and orange.

Mama gave me the eyebrow when I came out of my bedroom.

"You're going to draw a lot of attention to yourself in that," she said.

"Mama, let it be."

"Don't you tell me to let it be."

"I just want to have a good time."

"Brianna!"

We both stopped and stared at each other.

"Nothing is going to happen, Mama," I said. "I'm going to an art show. Van and those other boys probably don't even know there is an art museum in Reno. I'll be safe; I know it."

She nodded and closed her eyes. "You look beautiful," she said. "I just want you to stay that way."

CHAPTER FIFTEEN

CHEYENNE WAS A HOOT AT THE SHOW, WHICH helped lift me out of the pit I was sinking into. She was all dressed up in an outfit her foster sister Ellie, the cover girl wannabe, loaned her. The mini-jumper and turtleneck were fine, but the chunky-heeled loafers were too big, and Cheyenne kept walking right out of them every time she flung herself from one painting to another, which was about every ten seconds.

After the sixth time, Marissa picked up the shoes, grabbed Cheyenne by the arm, and said, "Let's go in the bathroom and stuff some tissue in these things before we get thrown out of here."

After they disappeared I really started to get into the exhibit. I'd never been to one, except for the shows we did ourselves at school and a sidewalk deal they had in Oakland one time. This blew me away. I forgot Cheyenne, forgot Marissa. For about an hour, I even forgot Van Hessler and the skinheads.

Two paintings by Henry Ossawa Tanner were locked up behind glass, that's how precious they were. *The Banjo Lesson* and *The Thankful Poor.* They both looked like dreams, as I stared at them. Yet they had that all-too-real feeling I'd had myself. I just never knew you could get it on a canvas like that.

Some pieces were by Aaron Douglas and August Savage,

both from the twenties. But the way they portrayed the down-and-out African-Americans of their time, they could have been painting the day before, right down in East Oakland.

What stopped me smack in my path, though, was Romare Bearden's work. I'd never seen anything like that. He took bits of photographs and colored paper and arranged them on a flat surface with paint. They turned out like stained-glass collages, all tiny pieces of things that somehow fit together, like he was making it up as he went along, and then discovered it when he was through.

I stood there gazing at one of them for a good ten minutes before I noticed the quote by him on the wall beside it. "Whatever subject the artist chooses, he must celebrate it in triumph," he had written.

I looked back at the collage. It *was* like a victory somehow. Even though he was presenting African-American life as he saw it, there wasn't any of that "we're tired, we're cheated, we're desperate" stuff I saw in some of the other art.

I got real excited when I saw a couple of panels from Jacob Lawrence's *The Migration* that I'd seen in the art book. It was so much more impressive in person. I could stand there and examine his solid-colored panes and then step back and see it as a cubist whole. I didn't like it as well as some of the other things. It left me kind of cold. I looked to see if there was a quote from him, and there was.

"You bring to a painting your own experience."

I smiled to myself. That would explain it. I didn't see things in cubes.

I stopped, though, when I came to the next one. *Tombstones* it was called. Only it wasn't a cemetery—it was a painting of the front of a tenement house. He used those same solid, primary colors, and at first it looked like a little kid had done it. But the closer I looked, the more I saw in it. A lot of death was in that project-house, but hope was there, too, in the way the figures were standing, the way they kept on holding their heads up even though they were living right in the middle of a graveyard. They were still trying; you could see that.

I came to a display of photographs next, and I almost skipped that, but then I saw that they were pictures of murals artists had done, like at the Harlem YMCA and Atlanta University. I tried to memorize names like Aaron Douglas and Hale Woodruff, the guys who produced art on a large, city-size scale. But nobody, it seemed to me, had done it like the Africobra artists, the ones who had done a street wall mural in Chicago called *The Wall of Respect*.

A quote was displayed next to that one with no name on it. It just said, "The power of art when it has the power of the heart."

How do they do that? I thought as I went back to look again at *Tombstones*, Bearden's collages, and the photos of the murals. *How do they get that power?*

It was like they had some kind of connection I hadn't gotten onto yet. It made my face kind of burn, thinking about the show I had up in the library.

"This stuff is cool!" Cheyenne said behind me. "Did you see that weird sculpture thing over there? It's made out of stuff the guy found in a junkyard."

I shook my head as I continued to stare at *Tombstones*.

"You're into this, aren't you?" she said. "I can only stand there and look at one for so long, and then it's 'next!'"

"What are you seeing, Brianna?" Marissa said.

I shrugged, but I knew. I just wasn't sure I could put it into words.

"Maybe you don't see it because you're white—and Latino—but to me, this is . . . eloquent."

"What does that mean?" Cheyenne said. "We had it as a vocabulary word, but I don't remember. Don't tell Norie, though. She gets all over me when I just memorize the stuff for the test. She says language is like this powerful tool or something, and you have to have a command of it—"

"So you're saying this art is like that," Marissa said.

"That's what I'm saying."

"So what's it talking about?" Cheyenne said.

"The plight of my brothers and sisters."

"I didn't know you had any."

"She's talking about her race," Marissa said. She looked at me, and I grinned at her with my eyes.

"What does 'plight' mean?" Cheyenne said.

"What's happened to them, how they have to live because of that. It stirs people up to want to do something."

"Oh," Cheyenne said. "Like your mouth painting did."

"Mouth painting?"

"Your *Voices of Violence*," Marissa said. She smiled a shy smile. "I go in and look at that every day."

I looked at her in surprise.

"That's what stirred up all this stuff with Van Hessler and those guys," Cheyenne said. "They didn't like your painting."

The energy of the art around me seemed to drain. "It was the wrong stuff to stir up though," I said woodenly. "Come on, we better go."

I was leading the way to the door when Marissa touched me on the arm in that I'm-afraid-you'll-bite-my-head-off way she had. "I don't think it was the wrong stuff to stir up," she said. "I just think they handled it the wrong way."

"They—you mean Van and them," Cheyenne said.

I shook my head. "Ira, too. Neither one of those boys would be lying in that hospital if he hadn't gone up there with them. That wasn't the way to do it."

"What is the way?" Cheyenne said.

"I don't know, girl," I said, as I pushed open the front door. "If I knew, I think I'd paint it."

"How would you do that?" Cheyenne said. "I sure couldn't. I'd get about two stick figures on there, and that would be it. I can't even color in the lines in a coloring book. Maybe that's because I didn't go to school until I was in fifth . . ."

I blocked her out. After what had just come out of my

mouth, I didn't want to say another thing until I'd worked that around in my mind. *If I knew what to do to stop the racial hatred and what it did to us, I'd paint it.* Where had that come from?

I was operating on automatic pilot as I took my keys out of my purse and stuck them in the lock on the passenger side to let Cheyenne and Marissa in. Maybe that's why I didn't see the boys until they were right there on us, standing too close, smelling too foul, breathing too hot in our ears.

"Give me the keys," Van hissed in mine. Then he took them right out of my hand, stuck his fist in my back somehow, and steered me to the other side of the Toyota. The way they did it was so slick—got Marissa and Cheyenne inside, unlocked my door, and deposited me in the driver's seat like a mannequin—it left me cold. I had the key in the ignition at Van's command before I realized that Dillon's brother was in the seat beside me and Marissa was down on the floor, curled up in a little ball. Van was right behind me, and Cheyenne was next to him with Garrick holding his hand over her mouth next to the window in the back. Her eyes were wild. I came to.

"What do you think you're trying to do?" I said. My voice was high and demanding. It didn't faze Van.

"We're taking you for a little ride. Well, actually, you're taking us."

Garrick snickered.

"Huh-uh," I said. "And who's going to make me?"

"I think I am," Van said.

I turned my head to give him an I-don't-think-so stare. Then I saw it, glinting in the sun like the nasty gleam in his eyes. A knife, pointed at my throat.

I looked at it, at him, at the window. The museum was on a quiet street. Not a car was passing, not a person was on the sidewalk. Even the birds seemed to have left the neighborhood. It's funny the things you think of at times like that. I just wanted to be out there, in the quiet, looking for birds.

"Head down California Street to Keystone," he said.

I stuck the key into the ignition. My hand wasn't shaking, but my mind was racing.

California Street. There would be a lot of traffic there. Maybe I could give somebody in a nearby car a sign or something. Van wasn't going to stab me in plain sight of a passing driver.

But one glance down at Marissa drove that idea right out of my head. Dillon's brother had a knife of his own pressing against her ear. He saw me looking.

"Don't get any ideas," he said. "Or her ear comes off."

Marissa didn't move. She had to be in shock, I decided. Not so Cheyenne.

I chanced a glance into the rearview mirror. Garrick still had her in a headlock with his hand firmly planted over her mouth, but her eyes were fiery now, and she was chewing him out in muffled tones. It sounded like the guy on the speaker at McDonald's drive-in.

I glanced back at the road, then into the mirror again. If she would look at me, I could encourage her with my eyes. If she did her usual thing, she could talk Garrick to distraction and maybe the other two, too.

Her eyes finally locked onto mine on my third check in the mirror. I nodded, just a little, and girl, my heart was pounding. She got the message though.

Without even hesitating, she screwed her eyes shut and took a big chomp out of Garrick's hand. He let go with a yelp that would have put a hound dog to shame. I slowed down so I could look and saw Cheyenne groping for the door handle. Yanking at the wheel, I jerked the car. Arms and legs flew up, and male voices cussed in both my ears.

I waited for the door to open. But as the car straightened, Cheyenne was still back there, and Van had her by the front of her jeans jacket.

"You do that again, and the beaner buys it."

I pulled up to a red light and looked down at Marissa.

Dillon's brother had the knife right up to the skin behind her ear. She still wasn't moving. I was certain she had passed out.

"He'll do it, Cheyenne," I said. My voice sounded calm—almost dead.

As the light turned green, I caught another glimpse of Cheyenne in the mirror just before Garrick shoved her back in the seat. Her eyes were flashing, and as I had hoped, she started to talk.

"You really think you're bad, don't you?" she said. "What's the big deal? So you can overpower three girls. Wow. What studs. I can't wait to tell all my friends—they'll all want to date you. Except my brother, of course. He'll want to smash you."

I could feel Van stiffening behind me, and I knew Garrick was probably doing the same. But nobody was going to chance putting his hand over her mouth again.

"You got a rag in here?" Van said.

"No," I said.

"So where did you steal the knives?" Cheyenne said.

"Shut up," Garrick said.

"Nobody would sell them to you, that's for sure. You look like a bunch of losers. Losers with shaved heads, that's all you are."

Keep talking, Cheyenne, I thought. I never thought I'd ever think that.

At the intersection of Keystone and California, Van hunched up close to my neck, sending a repulsed shiver down my spine.

"Take the freeway west," he said.

Good. We would encounter a lot of traffic between here and there. Somebody was bound to notice that Cheyenne was struggling like a tied-up bronco, and that I was probably looking, well, like a hostage. I tried to anyway. But Van was way ahead of me.

"Laugh," he said.

"Nothing's funny," I said.

The knife touched my neck. I could feel the point, pressing, just before breaking through. My heart felt like it had already been cut, and I could only imagine how Marissa must feel.

I opened my mouth and managed a hard guffaw.

"Keep it up," Van said. "You, too, Zach."

Zach. That must be Dillon's brother's name. He laughed mechanically, like it wasn't something he did too often. He didn't look like the yuck-it-up type. He was older than the other guys and more beat-up looking and pinched—the way people always look when they have smoked too many cigarettes and too much dope and awakened too many mornings with a head like a set of bongos. It was obvious from the crouched way he moved that he had been yelled at, whipped, and torn into so much as a kid, he was ready to do it to anybody who gave him a chance, before they could do it to him.

"Come on!" Van said.

I put on a big ol' plastic smile. "That was a good one, wasn't it, Cheyenne?" I said.

"No. I hate these guys. I'm not laughin' for them! Ow!"

"What did you do?" I said. "What did you do to her?"

"He bit my ear! Gross!"

"I'm *doing* what you say," I said. I gunned the motor ahead to prove it. "You don't have to hurt her."

"If anybody recognizes you, they're going to know you're up to something," Cheyenne said to Van. "Everybody knows you would never hang out with a black chick."

"Shut up!" Van said.

"No!"

The knife tightened on Marissa's ear. For the first time, she flinched.

"Here, stuff this in her mouth," Van said.

I looked frantically in the mirror. Van balled up Cheyenne's brochure from the gallery and handed it to Garrick. Cheyenne's voice went up into a howl, but no words were coming out.

That was when every hair on my head stood up, and my cheeks started to burn. I gripped the steering wheel and jammed my foot down hard on the gas pedal. If there was a cop within ten miles, he would be on me in seconds. Out here on the freeway, I'd be easy prey. And this time I would be glad to have them flatten me and my passengers against the hood of the car.

"Take the first Verdi exit," Van said.

My heart sank. Nobody would be on those roads.

What if I deliberately missed the exit? What if I just kept going—

"Slow down; you're turning here," Van said.

On the floorboards, Marissa gave her first whimper.

I took the exit, and cringed away from Van's pot-foul breath next to my face as he directed me down first one dirt road and then another. With every turn, we moved farther and farther away from houses, buildings, people. We were headed straight up into the hills.

"Where are we going?" I said. "This isn't a four-wheel drive, in case you didn't notice. I can't go much farther."

"You'll go far enough," Van said. "We're almost there."

Cheyenne mumphed, and Marissa was still. I couldn't give in. They were working too hard.

"Where is 'there'?" I said.

"The scene of the murder," he said.

I forced myself to roll my eyes. "What murder?"

"Dillon's murder," Zach said. He turned leaden eyes on me. "He died this morning."

CHAPTER SIXTEEN

THAT WAS WHEN I STOPPED BEING MAD AND STARTED being afraid. Very afraid. I'd seen eyes like Zach Wassen's looked now. I'd seen them in my mama the day Prentice died. And I'd seen them in the mirror. The eyes were looking at me with the kind of hatred that wanted revenge.

The Ford bounced painfully over a rock, and I put my foot on the brake.

"Keep drivin'!" Van said.

"It's too bumpy," I said. I hoped he couldn't hear the new strain in my voice.

"Keep going!"

"Then pull that knife away from her ear a little! You're going to cut her accidentally!"

"Good!" Zach said. He gritted his teeth and pressed the knife tighter. I could see the skin turning white beside the blade.

I stood on the brake and straddled a rock that pointed up out of the road. The knife pulled away—but only slightly.

"Ow! Oh!" Garrick let loose with the most cuss words per cubic inch of air yet. I saw his head go down below the mirror's level.

"What's the matter?" Van said.

"Oh, man!" Cuss, cuss, cuss.

I caught Cheyenne's triumphant eyes in the mirror. She

must have managed to get him good between the legs with an elbow or something.

"Take the left fork," Van said. It wasn't bothering him any. He had a mission, and it was burning right up my backbone. I was trying so hard to keep my hands from shaking that the skin under my fingernails was turning blue as I clutched the steering wheel.

The road he had pointed to went up at about a forty-five degree angle, and it was littered with rocks.

"I'm telling you, this isn't your Cherokee," I said. "This car won't make it."

"That's okay. We're getting out right up here. Just pull off."

I steered the Ford into a clump of sagebrush and tried not to stop too fast. The picture of that knife going into Marissa's head was painted vividly in my mind.

The one next to my head disappeared as Van turned to Garrick. I looked at Van sideways. For the first time, he seemed like he didn't quite know what to do.

Garrick was still doubled over and groaning. Ira didn't put up that much of a fuss with two broken legs and a fractured neck.

"You're about worthless," Van said to him. "Get up!"

"Can't!" Garrick wailed.

"You gotta stay here with these two while me and Zach take her." He jerked his head toward me.

Garrick looked up at Van, his face pea-soup green.

Van swore and turned to Zach. "You're gonna have to stay in the car," he said.

The knife came away from Marissa's ear in a flash of steel.

"No way!" Zach said.

"I can't leave him with the two of them! He's about to puke."

Zach wasn't having it. He came up over the seat with his face purple, and he and Van yelled things at each other that I won't pass on. I only heard about half of it anyway because my head was coming apart with thinking.

It wouldn't take anything for me to open the door and start running while they were arguing. As entangled as Zach was with Marissa, and Van being in the back, it would take a good fifteen seconds for either of them to get out of the car. I would have a major head start.

But there was no way I was leaving Cheyenne and Marissa. Unless I could signal them somehow.

But Van didn't give me the chance. He lunged over the seat and snatched my keys out of the ignition.

"Hold her," Van said to Zach.

Zach's fingers curled around my arm, and I didn't even try to pull away. He had a mean grip—meaner than Van's.

As Van exited, he pulled Cheyenne out with him. He stuck her head under his armpit and stomped to the back of the car. I could see her twisting and turning like a cat in a bag, and then I heard her yell loud and clear.

"Don't you *touch* me, you insane jackal!"

She must have gotten the ball of paper out of her mouth rubbing it against Van's side. It gave me a flicker of hope. One that lasted only until Van opened the trunk and pulled out the greasy rag Mama used on her hands when she checked the oil. He crammed that into Cheyenne's mouth, and not a sound came out. Her eyes were shooting sparks, but that didn't bother him. He picked her up by the back of her jeans jacket, dropped her into the trunk like a bag of dog food, and slammed the lid.

I went for the door handle then, but Zach stuck the knife right up in my face, so close I could see myself in the blade.

"Garrick, get up, dude," Van said. "You gotta watch the beaner."

Garrick turned damp eyes up to Van. "Can I have a knife?"

"Sure," Van said. But he was shaking his head and silently showing Garrick how to put his hand in his pocket and hold it against Marissa so she would think a blade was still there. I toyed with the idea of shouting, "He's not armed, Marissa!"

But I didn't like the look in Zach's eyes. He was going further and further out of control.

Van jerked his head at Zach, who got out of the car and gave his place to Garrick. The boy was moving slow, and he made a pain-face with every step. He was pathetic.

Van opened my door and yanked me out by the arm. Zach took the other one, and they headed up the road, hauling me between them. My feet weren't touching the ground, and their hands were digging into my arm muscles.

"Let me walk!" I shouted at them.

But they were on a roll. They got me to the top of that mountain, and they thrust me out in front of them to the edge of a cliff. Reno swam below me—far below. Beyond the harsh, brown mountains, cars were swarming like ants, and the neon lights that were on even during the day chased above the casinos, all too busy to know that I was up here in a howling March wind that was blowing away all my hope.

I had never felt so helpless. The skinheads had gotten their way. In a moment, in one step, I *was* going to disappear.

The sensation was so strong, I went limp between them. They kept holding on, kept squeezing tighter with every sentence that came out of their mouths.

"Your boyfriend, your *I*-ra," Zach said. "He killed my brother."

"He said let's have a contest for time," Van hissed through his teeth. "Whoever can get his vehicle to the top in the least amount of time wins. Only he didn't play by the rules. When he got to the top, he turned right around and came back down."

"He knew Dillon was heading right up there; he knew it. But he just kept going."

"Dillon flashed his lights, blew his horn. But your boyfriend didn't care. I was there." Van pointed off to the side of the road near the top. "I was right there. I heard your 'hero' gun his motor. I saw the look on his face."

"He thought Dillon would back down, go off the road,"

Zach said. "But he couldn't, man, and he got killed in cold blood by a dumb, ignorant . . ." He went off into the bitter jargon of a person whose only emotion is anger.

I knew. I used to talk that way myself after Prentice. Mama had brought me to Reno so we could both get away from that.

But I was never going to get away. Not ever. It was always going to be there.

"He's going to jail, Ira is," Van was saying.

"He'll do time," Zach said. "You ever known anybody who did hard time?"

I didn't answer. He didn't expect me to.

"Course you do; you all do," Van said. "Which is why everybody will believe you came up here to kill yourself. You *knew* what was going to happen to your man, and you couldn't stand it."

I understood what he was saying, but it didn't seem real. Either that or I was ready to cash it in. After all, what was the point? It was too big. And I was too powerless.

They wrenched me by both arms, splitting me almost in two directions. The edge of the cliff crumbled beneath my feet.

"You stood here, and you closed your eyes, and you just went." Van jerked me severely. My knees buckled, but I didn't fall. They were still holding on to my arms.

"Scary, ain't it?" Zach said. "Now you know how Dillon felt when that truck hit him, when he knew he was gonna go flyin' through the windshield and get under that African's truck." He gave me another jolt. "Just like that."

This time Reno swirled below me as my head and shoulders hung suspended over the city.

Van pulled me back. Zach was slower. I stumbled, and I didn't feel like getting back up. I couldn't make myself move.

Until I heard the scream from the side of the hill.

It wasn't Cheyenne's holler. It was rich and whole, and it tore right through me.

That was Marissa.

Something kicked up in me then. Maybe that last piece of anger that hadn't quite sagged out of me.

I swiveled toward Van and got my knee up. He dodged it, and I got him in the thigh.

Zach pulled me back, and I could feel something in my arm rip, but I didn't turn back. Gathering saliva in my mouth, I threw my head back and came forward with a wad of spit, right into Van's face.

His shock lasted long enough for me to take Cheyenne's cue and turn and bite the wrist of the arm that held me. The instant Van took it away, I got my leg up and shoved him with the bottom of my foot in the chest. He staggered backward and fell sprawling against a rock.

I turned to wrench my other arm away from Zach, but he got me from behind with both arms and pinned me against him. The city came up from the cliff again, and I stared down at it in horror. He was going to drop me, but I didn't want to go. I wasn't ready to give up yet.

Just as sharply as he had thrust me forward, Zach pulled me away and hurled me to the ground. Gravel burned through my chinos, and I caught my breath as the ground thudded it out of me. I wasted no time trying to scramble up, but Zach was standing over me. He planted his foot on my collarbone and pressed down. I lay on my back like an over-turned turtle.

I kicked up with my legs but they found nothing. Zach lifted his arm high up behind his head and I forced myself not to cringe. If he came down to hit me from that height, I could roll away. I could do that.

Except it wasn't a fist he threatened me with. It was a rock.

It was too big for one hand, and he brought the other one up and grabbed hold. Slowly, he poised it over my face. There was no unreal feeling. It was as horribly real as anything that had ever happened to me.

"I wouldn't kill myself by dropping a rock on my face!" I shouted at him. "This won't look like a suicide."

"Like I care!" he said.

He let go of the rock. I twisted my face to the side and screamed. The thing slammed to the ground, four feet away.

Zach looked down at me, his face opened in a gash of a leering grin.

"Made ya look," he said.

I rolled over and clawed at the ground to get up. I felt his foot come down again, this time right in the center of my back. He pressed it down, hard, then again.

"Hessler, get up!" he shouted.

"No, man, I can't. I'm sick," Van answered. "I hit my head when she shoved me. Man, the world's spinnin'."

Then I heard Zach swear—a loud, explosive sound, just before I heard a heavy thud beside me. I rolled back over and sat up. Zach was flat on the ground, face buried in the gravel.

"Oh no!" somebody said.

I looked up. Marissa was standing there holding a tire iron, her eyes stunned at herself.

"Oh no," she said again. "I think I killed him."

Van let out a string of expletives, the least of which was "witch!" He got to his feet and weaved toward us. "Stupid beaner witch!"

On the ground, Zach moaned. Marissa looked at me in horror.

"He's not dead," I said. "Listen to him whining like a baby."

That wasn't the only sound. Down the side of the mountain, it sounded as if someone was running through the sagebrush.

"There she goes!" Marissa cried. "There goes Cheyenne!"

I could have shoved that ball of paper in her mouth. Zach got his bearings and wove off to the left, down the side of the mountain. Marissa grabbed my arm and yanked me up.

"Come on!" she whispered.

"We can't leave Cheyenne!" I hissed back.

But she shook her head and kept dragging me down the

road toward the car. Cheyenne sprang out from the underbrush to my right.

"It worked!" she whispered loud enough to be heard in downtown Reno.

"Here!" Marissa said.

She thrust the keys into my hand and scrambled around the car to the passenger side. Cheyenne started to jump in the back and then stopped.

"Oh man, I'm dead!" she said.

"What's wrong?" I said over the top of the car.

"I lost one of Ellie's shoes!'

"Get in!" I said.

She leapt into the back while I yanked open the driver's door and started the engine. In a spray of dust and gravel, I backed the car up and jammed it into first. The back tires slid sideways as I gunned down the mountain road.

"Are they coming?" Marissa said.

Cheyenne got up on her knees in the backseat and looked out the window.

"I can't see yet. But who cares? They'll never catch us on foot!"

"Unless I roll this thing!" I said.

I'd never done any back-road driving. Ira had taken me a few times, but it always scared me to death.

"Look out! Oh, my!"

I let the words hang in the air and just held on to the steering wheel as we came up over a hump and then dropped what seemed like straight down the side of the next hill.

"You got up it, you can get down!" Marissa said.

"Keep thinking that!" I said.

"Hey, they're standing at the top of the hill wavin' their arms!" Cheyenne said. She howled. "Like we're really gonna go back and pick them up!"

"Zach got up?" Marissa said.

"Yup. It's Zach and Van."

I wheeled the Ford around the last curve before the paved

road and glanced over my shoulder, though all I could see was dust.

"What happened to Garrick?" I said.

Marissa looked over her shoulder at Cheyenne, eyes popping.

"Don't worry about him," Cheyenne said.

I took a corner practically on two wheels and put my foot on the brake. We slowed to about thirty-five so I could look at them.

"What?" I said. "Where is he?"

Cheyenne folded her forearms casually on the back of Marissa's seat and said, "He's in the trunk."

CHAPTER SEVENTEEN

THE CAR SWERVED IN MY HANDS. I JERKED THE wheel, narrowly missing a clump of sagebrush.

"He's in the trunk?" I said. "How in the world . . ."

"It was so cool, Brianna. We were awesome!" Cheyenne grabbed the back of Marissa's seat and shook it. "Tell her how rad we were."

I took my eyes off the road long enough to stare at Marissa. She was looking shyly into her lap. "Well, I knew—"

"Tell her about how you got me out of the trunk. I'm in there with that big metal thing trying to pry . . . well, that comes later. Tell her about getting me out. I don't even know how you got loose from that Garrick dude, so tell about that part."

"Well, she would," I said, "if you would hush!"

Cheyenne clapped both hands over her mouth and nudged Marissa with her elbow.

"Go on," I said. I pulled onto the freeway and nodded to her. "Tell me what's going on. Why do I have that dude in my trunk?"

"I knew that wasn't a knife he was poking me with," Marissa said. "It just didn't feel the same."

"What was it?" Cheyenne said.

"His finger," I said. "Van showed him how—"

"So what did you do? I gotta hear this!" Cheyenne said.

It was practically hopeless, but somehow they both got their stories out, and I was able to piece them together. It seemed that when Marissa realized she wasn't being threatened with a knife anymore, she stuck her finger down her throat and threw up all over Garrick. He started to yell, and she was afraid the other guys would hear him, so she screamed to cover it up. That was what I heard.

He got out of the car with her partially digested breakfast all over him, and he started to retch himself. He turned around, doubled over, and Marissa ran to the back of the car to whisper to Cheyenne that she was running for help. There were the keys, dangling in the lock where Van had left them.

She opened the trunk to find Cheyenne wielding a tire iron. She had been using it to try to pry open the trunk lid, and she was ready to clout whoever was standing there. Marissa grabbed it from her and turned because Garrick was coming up behind her. He was still half-sick from being kicked in the crotch, he had just finished throwing up because he was grossed out, and he was in no condition to resist when she threatened him with it.

Cheyenne picked up part of the jack, which was also in the trunk and between the two of them, they were able to force him in. It wouldn't close though, because the spare tire was in there, too. Cheyenne hauled that out, and they shut him in.

At about that point in the story, it occurred to me that neither Van nor Garrick was as "bad" as they wanted everybody to believe. I was able to knock Van over myself, and it hadn't taken much for them to get Garrick under control. As much as I was shaking by then, it was a positive thought somehow.

Marissa went on to explain that just about then, they heard shouting from up on the hill. She ran up toward us, tire iron still in hand. Cheyenne followed with the tire and rolled it up as far as she could, and then shot it off to the side. When Zach heard it, Marissa told him it was Cheyenne, who was actually way off in the other direction.

"Pretty sly, huh?" Cheyenne said.

The girl didn't even realize what had almost happened to us. She still thought we were in a Disney movie. Marissa looked a little more like I felt—shaken and wild-eyed.

"Where am I going?" I said.

Marissa looked blankly at the freeway as it wound ahead of us, dotted with Saturday traffic.

"Wherever it is," she said, "I hope an adult is there." She looked right at me. "We have to tell somebody, Brianna. They were trying to kill you."

"I don't think so," I said. "Van acted like he was going to drop a rock on my face, but then he threw it aside. He held me out over the cliff as if he was going to push me over, but then he didn't."

"Yeah, but what if he had?" She pushed her hair behind her ears. Her voice was on the near side of tears. "I know you don't like Ms. Race right now, but she was right. We can't handle this by ourselves."

"We should go to her!" Cheyenne said.

I narrowed my eyes at her in the mirror.

"Where else?" she said. "Tassie isn't home. She's gone off for the rest of the afternoon."

"Just give me a second!" I said.

She clamped her mouth shut, and I drove without really seeing where I was going.

Marissa was right; Ms. Race was right. I had to accept that now. One person was already dead. One was still hospitalized, two were up on the top of a mountain mad as the devil, and we had one in the trunk.

And Cheyenne had a point, too—where else could we go? My mama was out of the question. She would start packing the minute I pulled up to the curb. Who else was there we could trust?

"She's been there for everybody who's been in trouble," Cheyenne whispered.

"No," I said. "Absolutely not."

Then, like it was some kind of cue, this banging started from the back of the car—like somebody was angry enough to bust his way out of there with his fists.

"He's getting mad back there," Marissa said.

I sighed. "Where does Ms. Race live?"

Cheyenne got right up in between the seats and started to bark out directions. It only took us five minutes to reach the shady, older neighborhood where all the majestic homes had been turned into classy apartments. I was surprised. I'd always thought she lived in one of those gated communities with a pool, a Jacuzzi, and tennis courts.

"That's her out front!" Cheyenne squealed in my ear. "Who's that guy?"

"That must be Mr. Wonderful," I said.

"Who?"

"Forget it."

I pulled up behind what was apparently the guy's midnight-blue Camaro. Ms. Race was standing next to it, talking to a tall, big-muscled dude with one of those faces some white guys have that is almost too handsome. You know, Tom Cruise hair, Richard Gere profile, Brad Pitt aura.

He saw us first, and he looked at us as if we were a carload of annoying Girl Scouts coming to sell cookies. But when Ms. Race looked up and it registered who we were, she made a dive for my car and leaned in the window.

"What's wrong?' she said. "Are you all right?"

Nobody had said a word, but she was reading our faces, and what she was seeing was scaring her. She opened my door and pulled me out by both arms. I must have looked worse than I thought I did.

"What in the *world* has happened? What is it?"

"Something wrong, Enid?" the guy said.

She didn't even look at him. She didn't take her eyes off my face, except to glance at Cheyenne and Marissa as they got out of the car and joined us.

"We're in trouble," Cheyenne said. "We need your help."

"You have it; you know that," Ms. Race said. She gave me a little shake. "Talk to me."

Somehow it wasn't as much fun telling the story this time. Cheyenne and Marissa got their parts out in bits and pieces. I was a little better, but not much. I knew Ms. Race understood though, when the horror started to come into her eyes.

"So you still have this kid in your trunk?" the guy said.

I nodded.

He looked at Ms. Race with one corner of his mouth going up. "Uh, I think we have to call the cops."

"I know, Curtis," she said. But she looked at me. "You do agree, right? This has gone way too far."

"I know," I said.

"I have a phone in my car," Curtis said. "I'll call."

Ms. Race finally let go of my shoulders and put her arms out to both sides. Cheyenne and Marissa came into them, and we all stood there against her. It was awkward. It was lame. It was safe. I fought down the thickness in my throat.

"They're on their way," Curtis said as he jogged all studly-like back over to us. "I think I better get the kid out of the trunk before he suffocates."

"I'm taking these three in the house first," Ms. Race said. "Can you handle him by yourself?"

Curtis gave a short laugh, like it had been pretty stupid of her to even ask.

As Ms. Race ushered us up to the front door, Curtis pounded on my trunk. "Okay, dude," he said loudly. "I'm going to open this up. You stay put until I haul you out, or I'll have to take you down. You got that?"

I rolled my eyes at Marissa. "Get down with your bad self," I whispered to her.

She gave me a soft grin.

When we got inside, Ms. Race sent Cheyenne and Marissa into her kitchen to warm up some soup. She made me sit down on her couch, and she piled a bunch of pillows up around me. I don't even remember what the place looked like that first time I was in there. I had a whole lot of other things to think about.

So did Ms. Race. She sat down on a big cushion at my feet and folded her hands on the couch, like she was trying to keep herself from touching me and hugging me the way I know she wanted to. It was like she was pulling herself back.

"You did the right thing by coming here," she said. "I know you probably don't care about my opinion on this, but I'm giving it to you anyway. This was smart."

"Thank you," I said.

"Are you nervous about talking to the police?"

I shrugged.

"Anytime you want to stop, if it gets to be too much, you just tell me, and I'll deal with them. You've had a traumatic experience—"

"I'll be fine," I said. I didn't have a soft spot for the cops, but girl, they were the last thing I was worried about.

"Hey, Ms. Race," Cheyenne said from the doorway. "Do you have any of those little-bitty crackers shaped like fish to have with the soup?"

Ms. Race shook her head, and Cheyenne disappeared. But Ms. Race kept staring at the door, like maybe it would tell her what to say next.

"I don't know what you need," she said. "This is usually so easy for me."

"What is?" I said.

"Knowing what to say to you girls. Having the right answers."

"There's a real good reason you don't have the answers for me, Ms. Race," I said.

She fingered her braid. "What's that?"

"Simple. You're not black."

She looked hurt, but she tried to laugh. "I can't help it,

you know! But, honey, I just don't think there's that much difference between the two of us or between you and Norie or Tobey or Shannon. Race doesn't mean that much to me— we're people."

"But this is *about* race!" I said. "Those skinheads only hate us because of the color of our skin. Period. You never had anybody do that to you so you don't know how to fight it."

"And you do?" she said.

It wasn't a sarcastic thing she was doing to me. Her face was puckered, like she really wanted to know. When the door opened, I could have kissed the ground. Curtis brought in a police officer, and Ms. Race didn't have to wait around anymore for an answer I couldn't give her.

The Reno police officer was tall and thin and had a fuzzy blond mustache. He actually asked me if he could sit down beside me. Ms. Race sat on the other side of me, just in case I needed her. As it turned out, I didn't.

The officer—Officer Langley, he told me—asked his questions in a soft, husky voice and listened with his eyes. He nodded while he wrote down what I said. He never looked at Ms. Race or at Curtis for corroboration or to send them an adults-only message. After ten minutes, I stopped gripping the piping on Ms. Race's sofa with my fingers. He never once asked what I was doing in *this* neighborhood.

Cheyenne and Marissa brought in soup, and we ate while they gave their statements. I sort of stared at mine and pushed the kidney beans around with the spoon. All I could do was listen to the story one more time—and feel the fight coming up in me with no place to go.

Marissa's father picked up her and Cheyenne, but I still had my car to take home. I called Mama at about three, but she wasn't in yet. Officer Langley said he would follow me home to make sure I got in without any further "incident." Before we left Ms. Race's though, he received a page. Van Hessler and Dillon's brother, Zach, had been picked up walking down out of the mountains into Verdi. They were in custody with Garrick.

"I'll be fine going home alone then," I said to Officer Langley.

He crinkled his listening eyes at me and rubbed his mustache. "Guys like that have friends," he said. "Don't know why, but they do. I'll give you an escort."

Mama must have seen me coming down the street from our window, because she was out on the sidewalk when we pulled up. She came running to me, but her eyes were glued to that patrol car.

"Is this your mother?" Officer Langley said.

"Yes sir," I said.

He nodded politely to Mama, and to me he said, "You're all right now?"

"Yes, thank you," I said.

"Brianna, what on earth? What is going on?"

"You want me to stay and confirm your story for her?" Officer Langley said.

I shook my head at him.

"You all go on inside then," he said. "I'll wait until you're in."

"Brianna?" Mama's lines were etched so deep you could have stuck an envelope in one of them. I took her arm and about had to drag her inside the building. She kept looking back at the police car like she expected Officer Langley to suddenly pull his weapon and tell us to "Freeze."

When we got inside, I told the story for what seemed like the fifteenth time. She listened like she already knew what I was going to say, like she had expected it all along, down to the last detail. One thing I was sure she knew was that Dillon had died. When I was through, she took both my hands into hers. Suspiciously, I pulled them away.

"What?" I said.

"I have something to tell you, too," she said.

I started to shake my head, slowly, then faster and faster. "Not Ira," I said. "Not Ira, too—"

"No, baby, he's not dead. He's doing real well. Only I don't think he wants to do so well now."

"Mama, what are you saying?"

"The police paid him a visit today, too. Koretta called me. They've charged him with manslaughter."

"No. Huh-uh. No."

"He has to appear in court for a preliminary hearing as soon as he's strong enough."

I sat back on the couch and tried to split apart the two opposite things that were happening to me. Part of me was throbbing with relief. Ira wasn't dead. He might go to jail, but at least he was alive. Funny how being hung out over a cliff puts everything in its right place.

Then there was the other part of me, the fight that was charging up through me from my heart right into my head. It was stronger than ever because Ira could go to jail. He had messed up his fight.

I couldn't just drop it now, could I? But what if I fouled up like he did? People were dying over this now. And that was all the more reason to fight even harder, but to do it right.

"I don't know what you're thinking, baby," Mama said. "But let me say this before we go any further: I think we should move on. Get away from here. Once something like this starts, it never ends—"

"No, Mama," I said. "I have to fight back. I want to."

Mama put her hand to her forehead. "How are you gonna do that? I just don't see—"

"I don't know—except for one thing I found out today. We can't do it by ourselves. We have to have help. We have to have prayer, and it doesn't matter whether it comes from black or white or whatever. Mama," I sat up and got real close to her. "Mama, we have to connect with God on this." I took a big breath. "And I think I know how to start."

CHAPTER
EIGHTEEN

MAMA LOOKED AT ME, REALLY LOOKED AT ME. HER gaze tugged gently at me, to please make her believe.

I grabbed her hands. "Today, when I was up there just knowing that boy was going to push me off the cliff or drop that rock in my face, two of the most scared little rabbits on the planet got in there and were waving tire irons at punks and biting dudes' arms and making themselves upchuck to save themselves and me. The only way they could do that was because they've been praying and because the rest of the Girls have been praying. They don't get it. They don't have a clue about what it's like to be you and me and Eden and Harlan and Ira. But they go on and pray anyway."

Mama nodded as if she was afraid to talk, afraid she would break my spell.

"We need more of that, Mama. We have to go to church tomorrow, and we have to come right out and ask those people to pray for us and Ira and everybody that's in this. We can't be worrying about what they're going to think of us. We *need* them. We have to connect."

"Is that going to keep you safe?" she said in a voice I could hardly hear.

"I have to believe it will," I said. "Just like that police officer who brought me home. I've dealt with the police before—that's a whole other story—but they weren't anything like him. He treated me like I was a human being. Now why do you suppose that is?"

"Because you *are!*"

"Because he believes in God—you could just tell it."

She looked so weary, so afraid. I put my arms around her, and she sagged against my chest.

"I don't want to lose you, baby," she whispered.

"Then help me," I said. "We can do this. We have to."

She was quiet for so long, I was sure her answer was going to be no. It was all I could do not to beg. But finally, she pulled away and put her hands on my face. Her look went into me, deep.

"This is how it's going to be," she said. "We'll pray. We'll ask for all the prayer we can, and then we'll see. But if you don't make any progress—"

"How long?" I said.

"I don't know . . ."

"Until Ira gets out of the hospital," I said. "I have to be here for his hearing. If nothing happens before then, if we haven't taken even a baby step toward stopping this, then I'll go without a fight, I promise."

It took her a minute to start nodding, but she did. Her eyes were misty, and she was swallowing hard, but she was with me.

Sitting in church the next morning, listening to Sister Jasmine Phelps belt out a gospel song like Mahalia Jackson, I realized that just a week ago, I'd been sitting in this same spot with Ira beside me, thinking about my art show that was going to open the next day. Just a week ago, my biggest problem had been whether anybody was going to like my little paintings of eyes and ears and mouths. Who knew it was going to be those same mouths that were going to leave me sitting here with my heart pounding in my ears while I waited for sharing time?

I closed my eyes and whispered a prayer. I wasn't connecting yet, but I was taking steps, baby steps.

When I opened my eyes, I could feel someone looking at me. I turned my head, and across the aisle I caught Mrs. Quao's gaze. She was all in ice blue, a tidy little turban and a suit with a long coat. It made her look elongated and cold. I shivered and looked away from her. Dr. Quao wasn't with her, just Koretta. Maybe I couldn't count on him anymore anyway. He had, after all, agreed that I shouldn't see Ira. I tried to wipe that away and hold on until sharing time.

When the Rev. Boyette finally asked who would like prayer, I was the first one up. I had to get this out before I exploded.

"Morning," I said.

My brothers and sisters all answered with bobbing charcoal and cocoa and salt-and-peppered heads. The old people smiled at me.

"There's been racial trouble at King High," I said. "Some of you may have heard about it."

There were varying murmurs.

"Ira Quao was badly injured because of it," I went on. "And another boy, Dillon Wassen, has died. Ira's been charged with manslaughter. Three other boys are in jail for trying to kidnap two of my friends and myself. The Brothers of X from Sutro are out for revenge. The white supremacists have revenge of their own to take. It will all be hopeless if you don't pray."

There was a stricken silence, as if I'd said a bad word at the dinner table.

But then Rev. Boyette began to nod. "And none of us can rest until it's settled," he said. He looked around the silent congregation.

I could feel Mama's pain as she stared at her gloved hands in her lap. It was going to be just as she had expected. They were going to look down on us.

But the Rev. Boyette's look turned to a glare. "Am I seeing judgment in the eyes of my brothers and sisters?" he said. "Is there somebody here who has never made a mistake, never took a wrong turn, never had a doubt?" He pulled his eyes across the congregation. "I don't think so. Our Jesus Himself had doubt. Now this child is asking for affirmation. True religion is more than singing, ladies and gentlemen! We can't just sing and get happy and go home. We have to reach out and fulfill human needs. Now somebody ought to say 'Amen!'"

"Amen!" said an old voice in the back.

Then there were more. "Amen" and "Right on" and "Yes, Jesus."

I sank back down in the pew and took Mama's hand, clammy even through her gloves. Across the aisle, Mrs. Quao leveled her eyes at me. They glittered coldly like the diamonds that swung from her ear lobes.

After church, people surrounded Mama and me, and just as many rushed up to Mrs. Quao and Koretta. I thought that might mean we would get away before she could get her talons into me. Think again, girl.

Mama and I were almost to the car, walking arm in arm, when we heard her pumps tapping the sidewalk and her bracelets jangling together.

"Allegra, wait just a moment please," she called after us.

Mama and I stopped and looked at each other. She was the first one to roll her eyes so I figured I was safe rolling mine back.

"Good morning, Winnie," Mama said.

Winnie Quao brushed that off like Mama had offered her inferior pâté. Behind her, Koretta cowered.

"What do you mean by airing our personal family laundry in public like that?" Mrs. Quao said.

"She didn't do it," I said. "I did."

Mrs. Quao's eyes smoldered at me. The whites of them looked blue under her turban, a monster blue that seemed designed to scare me. But I wasn't even shaking.

"We have to have prayer," I said.

"You want prayer for yourself, ask it for yourself."

"But it isn't just your laundry, it's all of ours, every person of color."

"You leave my son out of it. He's being taken care of just fine, thank you."

"Without God?" Mama said.

I wanted to pick her up and hug her right there.

"Prayer is a very personal matter to me," Winnie said. She put her hand, heavy with diamonds, up to her chest as if I'd threatened to rip off her clothes.

"Maybe to you," I said. "But that's a mistake."

"Uh-huh!" Mrs. Quao said, her voice rising to beyond-soprano. "And you know it all, isn't that right?"

I opened my mouth to say, "No, but, I'm sure God does, girlfriend."

But she gave us one more wounded look and turned around and tapped her way back up the sidewalk. Koretta hung back, looking from her to us just long enough for me to make a quick decision.

"Koretta!" I whispered.

She waited, eyes dropping at the corners.

"I'm sorry, Brianna," she said. "She's just so upset—"

"I know," I said. "But do me a favor."

She nodded eagerly.

"Tell Ira I love him, would you? I mean, if you don't think it'll upset him too much."

Koretta nodded and looked anxiously off after her mother. "I have to go," she said. "I'll tell him."

"She'll tell him that and more," Mama said when she was gone. "She'll fancy this story up good."

"That's okay," I said. And then tears came to my eyes "I miss Ira, Mama," I said.

"I know you do, baby," she said. She took my arm, and we went on to the car, and I swallowed back the thickness in my throat.

When I got home, I called Cheyenne and Marissa to be sure they were okay. Cheyenne said everything was fine, except that Ellie was mad at her because she had lost Ellie's shoe. Cheyenne said she had already called Tobey and Norie to tell them the whole story—now you know that didn't surprise me—and they were going to pray even more, and Wyatt and Fletcher and Diesel and even Felise, not to mention Tassie . . .

I thought I'd never get off the phone with her.

Marissa didn't fill my ear quite as much. She just said she had talked to Shannon and told her all about it, and she was praying, too. Marissa also offered to come over to get the throw-up smell out of my car.

"Girl, that is about the last thing I'm worried about," I said. "Shoot, let's just call it a souvenir."

She started to giggle, and then I did, too.

"I bet that finger-down-the-throat thing would come in handy when a boy got too fresh with you," I said. "You might have to teach me how to do that!"

I was still laughing when I hung up. Laughing made me feel connected to them. It was like I was craving that connecting. I think that's what got me to sit down and work on my paper for Ms. Squires about the art exhibit. It was the first homework I'd done all week. Only I forgot it was homework, I got so into it. About halfway through, I got an idea. It was so strong I put down my pen and stared at the wall, the wall that had the painting of Mama and Prentice on it.

The pieces, all of them—my argument with Ira, my discussions with Mama and Ms. Race, Shannon's bigot father, and Ira's black upper-middle-class snob of a mother, Tobey's questions, Norie's research, and Marissa and Cheyenne's bravery—all that, plus the fear—everybody's fear—mine, Van's, Garrick's, Harlan's, and Ira's. Even the terror Crispus was trying to hide in all that I'm-gonna-bust-your-tail talk. It was all a lot of different things coming together like it did in those paintings. It made sense. It didn't spell out answers; it just made sense. Maybe that was the most important baby step of all.

Mama took me to school the next day—early—and I went straight to Ms. Squires. She was looking puffy-eyed as she sat in her office over a cup of coffee the size of a Super Big Gulp. Not a morning person, that lady. I, on the other hand, was running over with energy.

"Here's my paper," I said, plunking it on her desk.

She looked at it blankly.

"And I have a question for you," I said.

She nodded.

"There was power in that show," I said. "I've never seen—or felt—anything like that. One of them had a quote next to it. It said, 'The power of art when it has the power of the heart.' I don't know who said it, but anyway, I know what they were talking about. What I want to ask you is, do you think I have that kind of power as an artist?"

"Good heavens," she said, setting her coffee cup down on the desk. "I thought you were going to ask me for a hall pass or something. I don't know if I'm ready for a question like that yet. I don't have enough caffeine in me."

When I didn't move, she sobered up her face. Then she pulled down the knot of hair and redid it, this time with two pencils.

"All right," she said finally. "Yes, you have that power. More than any artist I've ever taught, in fact."

"Okay then, do you think I could pull off a mural, like those Africobras did in Chicago, and like Aaron Douglas and that other dude, that Hale Woodruff?"

"Absolutely," she said. "It's an exciting thought."

Even out of her sleepy haze her little blue eyes started to sparkle.

"Then that's what I want to do," I said.

She took a long drink out of her cup. "And where are you planning to do this?" she said. "You can't just go to some freeway wall and start to paint—ask some of the taggers in our class. It's called defacing public property."

I shook my head. "I'm no tagger, Ms. Squires. This is going to be art."

"I have no doubt about that, but finding a venue in this town could be pretty close to impossible. I don't mean to discourage you—"

"You're not," I said. "I have some friends who love 'impossible.'"

I think she probably drained the whole rest of the cup after I left. I tore on out of there and went to the journalism room where Norie always hung out in the morning. She and Wyatt were already huddled in front of the computer, talking like they had big, important business to transact. Girl, I think I know how they felt.

"Hey," I said.

"Bri, our hero!" she said.

"We need to have a meeting," I said.

"Hi, Brianna," Wyatt said, his mouth twitching. "Nice to see you."

"At lunch today," I said. "Boys, too."

I gave Wyatt a look, and he held up both hands. "Wouldn't miss it," he said.

"Uh, Ms. Race, too?" Norie called after me as I sailed out.

"Especially Ms. Race," I said.

The morning passed fast. In my first two classes I was sketching like mad. When I got to art third period, I had several drawings to show Ms. Squires. She hunkered down over them and rearranged them and looked at them and rearranged them again.

"I like these," she said. "But I don't *love* them. I think you're trying to do too much. You need to look at some Keith Haring. He did some mural work in Harlem that's outstanding. I think I have a picture of his *Crack Is Wack* wall . . ."

She trailed off to dig through a stack of magazines. I felt somebody behind me.

"Were you up again all night last night?" she said.

I turned around to look at Rachel. She wasn't wearing her makeup, and frankly, you could hardly see her face. It seemed to all disappear behind the dark circles under her eyes.

I didn't answer her.

"I was," she said. "I don't think I'm ever going to sleep again."

"Why are you telling me this, girl?" I said.

"Because it's your fault. It's your fault Dillon's dead. It's your fault Van and them's all in jail."

"No," I said, "It is not my fault. But I *am* taking responsibility."

"You are not," she said. "You people never take responsibility. All you do is whine about slavery. You're too stupid to—"

"Don't go there," I said.

"Is that a threat? Because if it is, I have no problem meeting you after school and taking you right down—and I won't back off like Van and them did."

"I don't want to fight you," I said. "I just want you to respect who I am."

"I don't respect *anybody* anymore. Everything's a crock. I'm just hatin' life right now."

She looked like she was going to dissolve. She turned around and started back to her corner.

"Hey," I said.

She looked over her shoulder. "I thought you didn't want to fight me," she said.

"I don't," I said. "I just wanted to say I'm sorry about your boyfriend."

"Oh yeah, right."

"I am. I've lost mine, too."

"He didn't die."

"In a way he did," I said. "I have to do something about it, and I'm doing it for him *and* for Dillon."

"I'll believe that when I see it," she said.

"You better believe it, girl," I whispered. "Because it's going to happen."

I believed that, especially after the Flagpole Girls—and Guys—met in the theater lobby at lunch. We prayed harder than I'd ever heard us pray. Then we got right down on the floor, and Marissa pulled out her marker and her big paper, and we brainstormed a Plan of Action.

We covered the whole thing before the last bell to end lunch. I got up from the tiles feeling something unfamiliar. I had to paint a picture of it in my mind. All of us with our heads together. Cheyenne sitting up and hollering, she was so excited. Ms. Race nodding at me with her face puckered, like she was really trying to understand. Diesel nodding all serious with his brows coming down over his eyes. All of us holding hands and saying one more prayer.

I entitled that mind-picture "Hope."

I know that was why, when Norie's mom dropped me off at home that afternoon after school since Norie's car was still at the glass shop getting a new windshield, I didn't panic. I could just stand there as Crispus and those two gorillas he always traveled with and Harlan and James piled out of a tired-looking Oldsmobile at my curb.

They crossed the grass and formed a line with Crispus a little out in front like usual, as if they had practiced it. It made me think of some old Michael Jackson video I'd seen.

"What?" I said.

"You shoulda taken our help," Crispus said. "Maybe now you got some sense in you."

"What sense, boy?" I said. "All you did was stir up more violence."

"How else you think we gonna stand up to them skinheads?" Crispus said.

"I don't know," I said. "Maybe if I thought about it hard enough I could come up with something even stupider."

Crispus blew me off with some kind of macho hand signal. "You think you safe now just because Garrick, he's in the 'Berg."

"Wittenberg?" I said.

He nodded. "Them other two's gonna be out on bail by this afternoon. They got a funeral to go to tomorrow."

"They're being tried as adults," Harlan piped up. I guess he had to say something so he would feel important.

"What are you telling me?" I said.

"You just expect trouble tonight, sister," Crispus said. He jerked his head back.

"Yeah, well thanks for the warning," I said.

Then I went calmly into the building and up to our apartment. It wasn't overconfidence or being naive that kept me so at peace. It was the Plan of Action.

That night, Diesel came over with Wyatt. Diesel was going to drive Mama's car to his house, and Wyatt would drive Diesel's truck back for him.

"Your car will be safe in our garage," Diesel assured my mother. "And I might as well do a tune-up on it while I got it."

"I need it at seven o'clock tomorrow morning," Mama said.

"It'll be here," Diesel said.

That put the Ford out of harm's way. The skinheads, we knew, liked to attack people's vehicles.

But we didn't see hide nor hairless head that night.

Norie and Wyatt did spend an hour on the phone with me asking questions for the big piece they were doing in the paper.

"I feel like a total geek," Wyatt said at one point.

"What was your first clue, boy?" I said.

"No really, I thought since the civil-rights movement in the sixties, you all were fine. I had no idea all this was still going on."

"I wish I lived in your dream world," I said.

But I really didn't mean that. My world was shaping up just fine.

The next morning, I met Tobey at Mr. Lowe's room before school. She was already in there explaining to him that we needed help to draft a letter and to put together a presentation for the people at the Jack-in-the-Box.

"We have to get them to let Brianna paint her mural there," Tobey said. "That wall in the back is the perfect place."

"If it can be done, you two will do it," Mr. Lowe said. He sat back and put his index fingers under his chin. I could almost see his bald head smoking.

"All right then," he said. "Here's what I think."

We finished the rough draft in time for Tobey to run off to first period. I went on back to my seat in Mr. Lowe's room, and he went into his office. As the other students wandered in, he came out with a couple of books in his hands.

"I can't tutor Ira like you wanted me to," I said. "His parents won't let me see him anymore."

Mr. Lowe's eyes sagged at the corners. "I'm sorry to hear that," he said. "I thought you were good for Ira."

"He's good for me," I said. "He's had things I never would have dreamed of, never would have had the chance to do if it weren't for him."

"That may be," Mr. Lowe said. "But you have a lot going for you, Brianna. More than you realize. Which is why I want you to read some of these stories instead of *Hamlet.*"

"Man," said the guy in the next row, "no fair!"

"Race has its privileges," Mr. Lowe said dryly.

"I wish I was black," the dude said.

I covered up a smile and looked at the books Mr. Lowe put on my desk.

"Start with James Baldwin," Mr. Lowe said. "I think you'll like that excerpt from *If Beale Street Could Talk.*"

I didn't think I'd be able to concentrate, not with all I had going on. But the end-of-the-class bell startled me right out of my seat. I'd finished the Baldwin section and was into Jamaica Kincaid. I never knew my brothers and sisters could write like that. It had power—just like those artists, just like Mama's jazz. It connected.

I made some more sketches for Ms. Squires, and she said I was getting closer. At lunch I ran to the journalism room. Norie and Wyatt were typing at one computer, Tobey at another.

"This is the coolest letter," Tobey said to me. "All we have to do is decide how we're going to present it."

"It has to have power," I said.

Tobey looked at me. "With you talking? No doubt!"

Ms. Race was waiting for us after school, and she gave us each a peppermint to suck on as we went to her car.

"I always like these when I'm nervous," she said. She looked at me. "But you aren't scared, are you, Brianna?"

"No," I said. "Am I supposed to be?"

"We've all been praying," Tobey said. "Marissa and Cheyenne are at Marissa's right now, praying us through."

I didn't mention that Shannon wasn't. She had sat through the whole meeting the day before, not saying a word.

I held my head up real high. "We're all praying that everything will work out the way God wants it to."

Ms. Race gave me a long look before she unlocked the car doors. "I told you this once, Brianna," she said. "Be careful what you pray for; you might get it."

I just didn't see where that could be such a bad thing. I was so stoked when we walked into the Jack-in-the-Box and asked to see the manager, I didn't even *need* that peppermint. Tobey kept looking at me and smiling even bigger, like she was getting her courage from me.

The manager was a thirtyish guy with his shirttail half hanging out and two of those vertical worry lines engraved between his eyebrows. He smelled like French fry grease and acted like he was in a major hurry. But Tobey invited him to sit down with us, and he forced himself to do it.

"We have a proposal for you," Tobey said.

"I can't donate any food for school fund-raisers," he said. "It's against franchise policy."

"We don't need any food," I said. "What we need is that wall behind your restaurant."

I gave him the letter to read. Then, using the presentation we had planned out so carefully, complete with two of my best pieces from my show, we laid it all out for him. I would do it all during spring break—which started at the end of this week, Cheyenne had told us to be sure to put in—when he wouldn't have as much traffic at lunchtime. I wouldn't block any parking. I'd have plenty of help to clean up my messes. And when it was done, we would hold the unveiling celebration right there. A whole bunch of people would be there to buy spicy chicken sandwiches and curly fries because we were going to get an article about it in the paper the day before.

"You're talented," the manager said. "I don't think the owner would mind having some of your work out there. I could talk to him."

I could feel my heart starting to pound hard. Tobey squeezed my hand under the table.

The guy looked again at the paintings I'd brought. "Which of these are you going to paint out there?"

"Oh, neither one of these," I said.

"Oh?" The worry lines deepened. "What did you have in mind?"

"I'm going to do an antiracism work," I said. "Something powerful that will stir people up, make them think twice about their views on people of other races—"

The manager stood up and shoved his piece of shirttail into his pants.

"Is there a problem?" Ms. Race said.

He gave her a look that would have refried the burgers.

"You're darn right there's a problem," he said. "I've had enough 'stirring up' around here. This place has turned into another Watts!" He looked at me. "You want to put some nice art out there, I'm all for it. Might give the place some class. But if you want to do your political thing, you're going to have to find someplace else."

IF THE DUDE HAD SLAPPED ME IN THE FACE, HE couldn't have stung me more. I got up from the table like my legs were numb and jutted my chin out at him.

"Thank you for your time," I said.

"Don't think of me as a racist now," he said.

No, dude, I don't think of you at all, I wanted to say.

Instead, I swept past him and waited at the door while a stunned Tobey gathered up our papers from the table and Ms. Race watched the manager scurry back to his soggy fajitas. The three of us moved across the parking lot in a silence Tobey evidently couldn't stand.

"I can't believe somebody would be so narrow!" she said. "Yikes!"

"I can," Ms. Race said. She put her hand over her mouth.

"What's the matter?" Tobey said.

"I was about to say something really preachy like, 'Welcome to the real world, girls.' You would hate it if I said that, wouldn't you?"

"What I hate *is* the 'real world,'" Tobey said.

We got to Ms. Race's car, and she looked curiously at me. "Brianna, you can go ahead and explode now. Nobody's watching."

"I'm not going to explode," I said.

She climbed in the car and started up the engine. "I don't

see why not. This is important to you. You have a right to fall apart."

"I can't be doing that," I said. "I have battles to fight, and I'm not giving them up just because one dude wants to hide behind his French fries."

"Curly fries," Tobey muttered.

Ms. Race was quiet then, which didn't bother me. I had to think about where I was going to go next to find a legal wall to paint on, one that a lot of people would see, skinheads and Brothers of X alike. I'd been so sure this was going to work.

Ms. Race dropped Tobey off at her car in the King High parking lot. Tobey didn't seem to know what to say to me so I said it for her. "Keep praying, girl. We have more work to do in this town than we thought."

She gave me one of those dazzling smiles. "You got it, girl," she said.

"I'd love to take you home," Ms. Race said to me. "It'll give me a chance to say something."

That made me want to take the bus, but I'd promised Mama I would find a ride home.

"Sure," I said. So *bad* I wanted to add, "But please don't say anything; I have this all figured out finally. Please don't try to talk me out of it."

She waited until we were all the way down to McCarran before she spoke, all careful, like she was trying to make sure she said it right. It did occur to me about then that she was almost as uncomfortable with me as I was with her. No wonder she was always so condescending.

Finally she tightened her fingers around the steering wheel and said, "I was wrong, Brianna."

Now that stunned me.

"About what?" I said.

"I said it so many times, 'Brianna, you're just like the rest of us, we're all the same, we're equal.'" She looked at me with her eyes all soft. "But that isn't true, is it?"

"Depends how you mean it," I said.

"You have to be different, because you have different battles to fight. You're in a war I don't know anything about. I've never had to practically beg to be recognized for the person I am."

"I'm not begging," I said.

"I know. That's what makes you amazing. I just want you to know I was right when I said it was too big for us to deal with alone, and I still believe that."

I nodded.

"But I can't tell you how to fight the battle. I can't expect you to think and act and feel like white girls do because there's a huge difference. Yet I respect you every bit as much and love you as much, and I know we have equal rights to become all we can be."

She let out a huge sigh, one she had probably been keeping in since the first day we crossed swords. I have to admit, I felt pretty relieved myself.

"Thank you," I said.

She smiled, kind of sadly. "I wish there were more to thank me for. What I really wish is that I knew some rich building owner who would let you use his wall for a little while."

I felt like a guitar string being twanged. "Somebody rich?" I said.

"That's what we need. Somebody who has enough money to risk losing a little business for a good cause." She frowned. "If there is anybody like that."

"Yeah," I said.

We pulled up to my curb, and I already had the door halfway open. "Keep praying, Ms. Race," I said.

She looked a little confused as she drove away. But my head was clear. I marched right up to our apartment and went for the phone. When I dialed, Mrs. Quao answered. So far God wasn't doing it my way, but I plunged on.

"Is Dr. Quao there, Ms. Winnie?" I said. "I know this is his day off and—"

"He's taking care of some family business," she said in that which-you-don't-need-to-know-about voice.

I heard a male voice in the background. The phone muffled, like she was putting her hand over it.

"I just need to speak with him for a minute," I said. "And it isn't about Ira."

"Girl, I said he is busy!"

Again the male voice. I could plainly hear it saying, "Winnie, who is it?"

After a short silence, I heard the sound of the phone being passed from hand to hand.

"Hello?" came Dr. Quao's soft accent.

"It's Brianna," I said. "I'm sorry to bother you. I know I'm about the last person you want to talk to—"

"On the contrary! Why would you say that, my dear?"

Oh, no special reason—except that you've shoved me out of your family's life!

"Ira is doing much better," he said. "He is off all oxygen and such. Only one tube goes into his arm now. We all like that, yes?"

"I'm glad, Dr. Quao. I sure am, but that's not why I called."

"Oh?"

I closed my eyes and tried to see him on the other end, waiting patiently. Nodding and closing his eyes as I talked. Loving me with his soft face.

I took a breath and it came out—what I wanted to do, what I needed to do it. When I was finished, I held my breath again while he thought.

"I will see what I can do," he said. "I know some people. I will make some calls. Will you be home this evening so I can call you back?"

I wanted to crawl through the receiver and hug his neck. "I'll be here!" I said.

"Oh, now if you happen to be at the hospital, perhaps we could connect there."

I started to stammer. "Uh, no sir. I don't think I'll be there. I mean—"

"I wonder that you haven't been to see Ira in several days," he said. "A visit from you would certainly do him much good."

When Mama came home, she stopped in the living room to turn on some music and found me in the kitchen, still reeling from that statement. She leaned over to kiss my forehead and put a bag of groceries on the table. Jazz—Miles Davis on trumpet—electrified the air. For some reason, I felt a little bit happy, happier than I had been in over a week.

Mama glanced at me as she pulled some carrots, potatoes, and stew meat out of the bag. "You're looking mighty pleased with your sweet self, Miz Thang," she said. "What's happening?"

"Dr. Quao is still on my side," I said.

"I thought he was the one told Winnie you shouldn't see Ira."

"I don't think so. He just asked me why I haven't been to the hospital."

Mama stopped, potato peeler in hand. "Well, that woman! I tell you, baby, I do not *know* what we can expect of our children if the parents are going to manipulate people like that. Mmm-mmm."

She turned to the sink, still shaking her head. I got up to put away the rest of the groceries. Reaching up with the salt to put it in the cabinet above Mama's head, I swung my hips to the music and bumped her thigh. She laughed and bumped me back. In a minute, we were both getting in the groove.

"Oh, yeah," she said when I danced off to set the table. "You know why I love jazz so much, why it calms me down the way it does?'

"Huh-uh," I said.

"If you listen to it—I mean really listen to it—you can

hear how they're all in there doing their own thing, playing one note at a time. But they're listening to each other, too, and it all just comes together."

I stopped with a plate poised above the table. "You mean, they connect," I said.

"Mmm-hmm," Mama agreed. "I've been thinking about that all day. I took some Wynton Marsalis to listen to in the car and at work today because I knew I was going to be all jitters. And you know, that Jesse fella I told you about, the one who looks at me every day like I'm new there . . ."

"Uh-huh."

"He poked his head in my office door and he said, 'You into jazz?' I said 'Uh-huh.' And he said, 'It's heaven's music. Somebody told me you have to walk with the Lord to make music like that.'" Mama shook her head. "Isn't that something?"

I guess I answered. Mostly I was staring at the forks I was holding. Another piece had just fallen into place.

"Mama, do you mind finishing up?" I said. "I just got an idea, and I need to get it down before it disappears."

"That sounds like a good excuse to get out of cooking," she said. But she laughed and waved me on.

I pulled the sketchbook out of my backpack, and I sat down on the living room floor in front of the speakers, and I started to draw. Girl, it just flowed out of me, just like a good prayer does. In fact, I made a prayer out of the whole thing. It was like God was right there, telling me what to put down, not through words, but through my fingers. And I just kept draw-praying until it was there. All the pieces—all the people—came together. It was connecting.

I stayed up late, reading from one of the books Mr. Lowe gave me and waiting for Dr. Quao to call. He never did. I might have gone sliding down some, if it hadn't been for what I was reading. I put myself to sleep reading from *Betsey Brown*, and I about decided Ntozake Shange wrote like I wanted to paint—in colorful pieces that all came together in a whole. A hopeful whole. Besides, I finally found out who Seymour and Charlotte Ann were: childhood sweethearts.

I didn't know where to go first before classes started the next morning. I wanted to show my sketch to Ms. Squires, but I also wanted to tell Mr. Lowe how much I loved Shange. I decided on him, since Ms. Squires had a head like a bowlful of porridge first thing in the morning. I went flying past the office and running down the hall to his room. I'd barely arrived, when Ms. Race came in behind me, all out of breath like she had spotted me from down the hall and came tearing after me.

"Excuse me, Mr. Lowe," she said. Her eyes were sparkling like I hadn't seen them do in a while.

"Ms. Race," he said. "I don't see enough of you!"

"Then we'll have to do lunch," she said. "But I'm here for Brianna."

I looked at her sharply. She was holding out a pink piece of paper. "You've had a phone message already this morning," she said. "I just took it."

What was up this time? I took it from her like I expected it to bite me, but she didn't even give me a chance to read it. "It's from Dr. Quao," she said. "You know that car wash across from the Jack-in-the-Box?"

Everything happened fast after that. You talk about connections, girl.

I took my design to Ms. Squires. She didn't squeal—she's not that kind—but she folded her arms across her chest and said, "Now, yes. Yes. Yes. Yes."

I took that as a yes.

That afternoon I took it down to the car wash, this time with all the Flagpole Girls—except Shannon.

The manager down there, a dude named Femi, who was from Nigeria, didn't even wait for me to get halfway through my speech. He put his hand on my shoulder and said, "Yes, yes. You can do it."

He spoke English real proper, like he had gone to the same school Dr. Quao did.

"But I have one—what do we call it—stip—"

"Stipulation," Norie said. "What is it?"

She was ready to take it down on a notepad. I just listened with my eyes.

"You must be protected," he said to me. "There will be people who will want to destroy your art. I know this."

"You mean, like, a security guard or something?" Tobey said.

The girls looked at each other doubtfully. I just watched Femi.

"No, no. That is too crass. No, we must have some way to cover your work until it is ready to be revealed. And then, of course, there must be a dramatic opening."

What was this dude doing running a car wash? He was an artist himself!

"You're talking a tent or something," Norie said.

"Cool!" Cheyenne said. She nudged Marissa, who rolled her eyes at me.

"When will you begin?" Femi said.

"Spring break," I said.

"This Friday night!" Cheyenne said.

We all groaned.

"I will be ready for you," Femi said. "Godspeed."

Then he rubbed his hands together and hurried off to the little office attached to the bays where people were even then washing their cars. It was all too bizarre to question. I could only stand there and grin.

"Let's celebrate," Cheyenne said.

"Not yet." Norie tapped her pencil eraser on the notepad. "We have to come up with the cash to buy all Brianna's supplies."

Ms. Race reached for her shoulder bag. "I have about fifty dollars—"

"No," I said. "I can't do it that way. Not to be rude, but I can't just let you pay for it."

"I'm not paying for *this* painting, Brianna," Ms. Race said. "I want to buy one from your library show. I was thinking about *Voices of Violence*."

"I want that one!" Marissa burst out—and then she covered her mouth.

"Oh well, I can pick another one," Ms. Race said. "*Ears of Fear* is good."

"You mean, we can buy that stuff?" Norie said.

I nodded.

"My mother will freak," she said.

Mrs. Vandenberger did "freak" with her checkbook. She bought three of my paintings for herself, and when she found out how much Marissa wanted *Voices of Violence*, she bought that for her. Between that and Ms. Race's purchase, there was more than enough for all the paint and brushes and other supplies I needed. Marissa's father, who was in construction, supplied the scaffolding, and Ms. Squires helped me make a grid so I could paint my mural from my small rendering. Everything was set, except a way to keep me and the mural covered until the time to unveil it. Femi insisted on that.

We still hadn't come up with anything by Friday, the last day before spring break. I couldn't get myself to worry though. I just kept making a prayer to God, making pictures in my head of how this was going to be and what it might just possibly do.

"We're making progress, Mama," I said to her that morning when she dropped me off.

"Let's just wait and see," she said. "I don't want you to be disappointed."

I wasn't. That day at lunch, the school paper came out, and I didn't see anyone who wasn't hanging his or her head down over it while eating pizza or peanut-butter sandwiches.

Black Women Have No Feelings and Other Myths about African-Americans the headline read. Norie and Wyatt had taken all the things white people seemed to believe about my race and explained them away one by one. Things like:

Black males are responsible for nearly all the crime in America.

Black men are shiftless, can't be trusted, are never around when you need them, and won't respect or protect their women.

Black women are cold and tough and have no deep feelings.

Education is the great equalizer.

Everybody is treated equally now.

The rise of the black middle class is evidence that racism is dead.

It's totally okay to be black now.

I liked "Black women have no feelings" best. Under that one, Norie had written, "No, black women have just learned how to mask their thoughts and feelings because it hasn't always been safe, historically, to share their emotions. They have had to use denial out of fear that what they feel will be used against them."

Ms. Race liked it, too. At lunch, she sat next to me before we prayed, and she pointed to it, silently, and she squeezed my hand.

"No need to be afraid with me anymore," she said. "And I would love to know what you feel. I bet you out-feel us all!"

It was a baby step for sure.

That afternoon after school, to the tune of Cheyenne singing, "Free at last! Free at last! Thank God Almighty, I'm free at last," we all went down to the car wash—guys, girls, Ms. Race, the whole mob. We still didn't know how we were going to meet Femi's stipulation—at least I didn't. Some of them seemed to know something, however. Tobey and Norie kept giggling, and Wyatt kept telling them to hush.

"What's so funny?" Fletcher said as we were headed down MaeAnne, a bunch of us crammed into Tobey's Lazarus.

"You'll see," Tobey said.

And I did.

When we came down that last little incline at the corner, I looked over at Femi's place, and I just out and out gasped.

There, extending from the wall I was going to paint, to about six feet out and enclosed on either end, was a tent, a big, striped, canvas tent.

"Where did that come from?" I said.

Nobody would tell me. I was still asking when I got out of the car.

"It came from God, I guess," Ms. Race said, wrinkling her nose at me.

"No, not quite," Norie said. "My dad rented it for you—and he just *thinks* he's God."

While they were all telling Norie how horrible she was to say that, I crept over to my tent and peeked in. Not only had Dr. Vandenberger set up the tent, he had had lights hooked up using a giant extension cord that trailed across the parking lot to Femi's office. There was a whole power strip in there.

"In case you want to have a microwave, Jacuzzi, all that stuff," Wyatt said.

"I don't even know what to say," I said.

"I do!" Cheyenne said. "Let's do our thing we planned."

They all glared at her.

"You have the biggest mouth on the planet, Cheyenne," Tobey said.

But I knew mine was bigger. I just kept standing there with it hanging open while they gathered around me in a circle and put their hands on me. In a ceremony of prayers, song, and the presentation of a—as Tobey put it, "honkin' huge"—paint roller, they commissioned me to do God's work. I about cried. But Brianna Estes does not cry.

The next morning, 7 A.M., I was there in sweats, gloves, and a knitted hat to wear until the sun burned off some of the last-week-of-March cold. I started to paint.

I know I would have gotten lost in it, that day and Sunday, Monday, Tuesday, Wednesday, and the rest, if it hadn't been for the kind of support I had every day, almost every hour.

The Girls took turns bringing food. Everyone except Shannon. Marissa kept apologizing for her, until I told her there was just no need. Then we all, conspicuously, didn't mention her at all—until the day Tobey brought me a sandwich from Port of Subs and then left. When I opened it, there was an envelope with a letter inside.

Dear Brianna, (it read)

I don't think I've ever been so miserable in my whole life. Everybody is helping you, and I'm not allowed to. It's my dad who won't let me. He keeps telling me there will be nothing but trouble coming out of this. Personally I think he's prejudiced—not to talk bad about my father, but I think he is. But I wanted you to know that even though I can't go against what he says and I can't come over there and bring you cookies or something, I am praying for you. And for me, too. I'd give a lot to be as brave as you are.

Shannon

I made a prayer out of that, too. At least I was allowed to believe what I knew was truth. I gave thanks, and I prayed for Shannon.

The Guys took turns just being around, in case there was trouble. Until the paper came out on Saturday, nobody even knew what was going on. A few curious people would come out of the washing bays with their dripping cars and holler, "What's happening?" and Diesel would growl at them or Wyatt would just smile and wave them on or Fletcher would make up some cockamamie story about incubating chickens, and they would just drive off.

Norie brought me her cell phone in case of an emergency, and Ms. Race came by the first day with a boombox so I could have music. Mama even got into it and gave me a whole stack of her precious jazz. The whole time I was painting, I was listening to Charlie Parker, Billie Holliday, Duke Ellington, and the Miles Davis Quintet and remembering what Mama said about the music. If my brothers and sisters in the music world could make their prayers that way, I could paint that way.

One of my biggest surprises was Ms. Squires. She came by every day around three to see what I'd done during the day. She gave me some critique, even some help that last day when I was nervous about finishing. Mostly though, she just stood, looked, and watched me work. Once in a while she would say, "Yes."

But the very biggest surprise was Mr. Lowe. Friday afternoon, when I was getting real close to finishing, he poked his head in the tent with his bald head shining in my lights.

"I didn't come for a preview," he said. "I won't look, if you don't want me to."

"No, Mr. Lowe, you can look. I want to know what you think."

He never did say. He just looked at my mural, and his eyes misted over.

"I told you once it had been a long time for me," he said.

I paused with my paintbrush over the sienna. "What did you mean by that?" I said.

"My first teaching assignment—longer ago than I care to say—was at Booker T. Washington High School in Norfolk, Virginia. Needless to say, it had a mostly black student body."

"Uh-huh."

"I went in there thinking I was going to grace those kids with a superior education," he said. His bald head reddened. "*They* educated me! I wouldn't be the teacher I am—or the person I am—if it hadn't been for my work with those students. There's power in being a person of color—if you can just avoid the pitfalls." He squinted behind the glasses. "I'm sorry I didn't give you some help sooner, Brianna. I'd forgotten how to read the signals."

"You can help me now," I said.

"Oh?"

"I brought *Betsey Black*—in my backpack. You want to read to me a little while I work?"

It was one of my best afternoons. Charlie Parker in the background. My almost-completed mural before me. Mr. Lowe reading Shange from a chair nearby. It was heaven, right on earth.

Those were the treats and the surprises. The beauty though—that came every afternoon when Mama picked me up, and she took me to see Ira.

She was the one who brought it up, that first Saturday. She said, "Baby, there isn't much I can do to help you, but I can at least take you to the hospital and help you stand up against Winnie Quao. Where does she get off, anyway, telling *my* baby what she can and cannot do?"

She went off from there, and I tried not to smile all over it. She was the *best* Mama.

Mrs. Quao wasn't there when we arrived. Mama stood guard out in the hall while I tiptoed in and kissed Ira on the cheek. He opened his eyes, and, girl, he just started to cry.

"Baby, where have you been?" he said. "I thought you hated me. I just thought you were gone for good."

He wasn't making enough sense himself to be able to understand what went down with his mother. Sure, I was ready to chew up the bedpan because she had lied to me and because she hadn't ever told Ira a thing. But I was making more progress than even I knew. I was learning when to keep my mouth shut.

Queen Winnie didn't give in easily. She and Mama had it out in the hall—until a nurse came and told them to please take it outside, and then they did. I don't know what went on, but Mama won. After that, Mrs. Quao didn't come in during my visiting hour. It was Dr. Quao who told me on Friday that Ira might go home on Easter Sunday, just two days away.

"We'll have to have a nurse for him. He still needs a lot of care," he said. "But he'll thrive at home where you can come and see him anytime."

That was going to be a trip, but I put that worry on the back burner. I spent more time wishing that Ira could be there Sunday morning, when the tent came down. That was all right, I kept telling myself. The mural was going to be there for a long time, I hoped.

The day before Easter, at four o'clock, I made my last stroke. There was nobody there right then, except Diesel outside somewhere, making the parking lot safe for art. Bessie Smith finished up a song on the stereo, and everything got quiet. I stepped back as far as I could, and I looked.

The faces on the wall looked back—not guarded and fearful and militant and fighting for their supremacy, the way they were today—but yearning, burning with hope, the way I longed for them to be tomorrow and every day after.

I focused for a minute on the black faces. Had I captured them the way my model painters had humanized their subjects, the people who had stood on the slave ships and the auction blocks and the cotton fields and the factories? Had I done that?

The faces answered that for me—and the hands that reached out from the wall. I had expressed them more the way things ought to be than the way they were. I could do that now—I didn't have to hide my feelings anymore. Those slaves and factory workers I'd seen in the paintings of Tanner and Bannister had paid for this moment—so I could tell the world how I felt about the way it ought to be.

Norie had said that once, that we were all paid for.

Paid for by God, that's what she had meant. And this was my connection, because I felt the very presence of my ancestors, of the painters, of the singers, and of the writers who had gone before me. Of God.

I'd made a prayer of it, and God was there. I knew that was the way I would always pray, from then on, no matter what happened when that tent came down tomorrow.

Then Brianna Estes put her face up to the faces that looked back at her from the wall, and girl, she cried.

EPILOGUE

THAT NIGHT, WHILE I SOAKED IN THE BATHTUB, mama read me the article in the *Reno Gazette-Journal* about the unveiling of my mural the next morning. She didn't tell me, until much later, that the phone had been ringing all day with people assuring her—and threatening her—that they would be there. People from the church. All the Flagpole Girls. Rachel. Crispus. Everybody but Winnie Quao, which only made sense.

All Mama told me that night was that she would be there with me. She kept the thought "because I know this is going to be a disappointment" to herself, but I could see it in her eyes. It was a good thing I was connected. I just made a prayer of it in my mind's eye.

Easter morning before dawn was an incredible thing. Although a nip was in the air like there always is in early April in Nevada, there was no wind. Reno without wind is about a miracle.

I wore a long, flowing, purple outfit Mama put together for me, and I felt magnificent. When we arrived, people were already there in their clumps. Our church family was ready for the morning's services that would follow later, all in suits and ties and big flowered hats, and they were waving to us. Ms. Race, Curtis, and the Flagpole Girls were there with their parents—all but Shannon.

Van Hessler, Rachel, and Zach were on one end of the

parking lot with a bunch of other boys who had weird things shaved into their heads.

Crispus and the two henchmen were on the opposite side, in their flashiest earrings. Harlan and James weren't with them. They were standing on the other end of the parking lot with Eden and Laraine. They looked like the new kids in kindergarten, until Cheyenne, bless her heart, invited them to stand with the Flagpole group. Harlan did it, of course. He would go wherever he was invited.

Ms. Squires was there, too, and Mr. Lowe, and of course, Femi. He had on the coolest Nigerian traditional costume made of kente cloth, complete with a kufi on his head. I was going to have to ask him where he shopped.

Everybody started to clap for Mama and me, and they didn't stop. They just kept clapping in rhythm, led by Sister Jasmine Phelps, naturally. The Girls really got into that. The skinheads and the Brothers of X stood stone still.

Everybody got still when Femi led Diesel, Wyatt, and Fletcher up to the tent to release the ropes. I sneaked one more glance at the skinheads, but they were watching the driveway. A police car was pulling in. I tried not to grunt. I tried to stay positive.

Which wasn't hard when the door opened, and Officer Langley unfolded his long ol' lanky legs out. I caught Ms. Race grinning and nudging Curtis. That was her doing.

Femi gave the signal, and Diesel, Wyatt, and Fletcher took hold of the ropes. Like a piece of gauze, the tent folded. My mural faced the world for the first time.

There was the longest silence since the whole beginning of creation, I know that. And it was a thick silence—heavy with all those thoughts, all those feelings as people met the faces of my painting.

Crispus was the first one to move. He stalked right up to the wall and glared at it—like he was commanding it to be something else. When he finally looked at me, he shook his head and jerked it at Ring Nose and the other one. Like a militant little no-brain trio of toy soldiers, they turned on their heels and marched away.

It wasn't what they expected. There was no fist of Malcolm X rising out of the mire of black suffering. There were no blood-spattered whites being hurled to hell at the hands of the superior Negro race. And the Brothers of X wouldn't accept anything else.

It was the skinheads I watched now. I'd never seen them look like that—so slack-mouthed, with their eyes released out of those slits. They were like baldheaded babies to me now.

I looked up at the mural, where the face of Dillon Wassen was looking back at them with the bright abstractness of his youth and energy. Vulnerable and real, he reached out to them, and with their eyes they reached back. They seemed not to see Ira up there or me. They didn't focus on the images of Marissa, Cheyenne, Crispus, Rachel, and Shannon, all of them on the wall reaching up and out with their arms until the trails of their limbs formed the word CONNECT. They just saw their brother. Rachel put her head down, and she cried. Zach tried to tighten his face, but he couldn't. Van just stared.

Then he jerked his head, and the three of them and their bald band left in silence. Theirs wasn't a bitter one though. It was a puzzled one.

It was all I could have hoped for. Whatever was going to happen now, I didn't know. But I was hopeful for what *wasn't* going to happen—at least not today.

I looked at Mama and smiled. She smiled back—the young smile I loved. "Baby step," she mouthed to me.

Officer Langley stepped up to me. "It looks like there isn't going to be any trouble at this point," he whispered.

"Yes sir," I said.

Cheyenne came running up to us, and I could see she was forcing herself not to blurt something out with the police officer standing there. He smiled down at her and stepped aside, before she popped. "Brianna!" she said, her voice squeaking. "Did you see who just got here?"

I followed her wildly waving hand to the parking lot. A station wagon I didn't recognize was backing into a parking space so that its rear end would face the mural. I looked at Cheyenne.

"Who is it?" I said.

She was jumping up and down, girl, by that time. "It's Ira!" she said.

It sure enough was. His daddy got out of the car and opened up the back. Ira was there, on a pallet, propped up with all his casts and neck things and paraphernalia, and he was staring at the mural. Even from there I could see the stars in his eyes.

"Go to him," Marissa whispered to me.

But I knew if I went right then, I'd never want to let him go.

"I will in a minute," I said. "But we have to do something first."

"Everybody over here!" Cheyenne shouted.

The Flagpole Girls came immediately, but I waved my arms over my head. "Everybody," I said. "I want everybody!"

We made a big circle, opened at the end so Ira could be in it, too. I had Mama on one side and Marissa on the other. Across from me, Cheyenne was between the Rev. Boyette and Sister Jasmine, talking their ears off.

"Somebody ought to say, 'Amen!'" I shouted.

And we did—and, girl—it was a prayer. A prayer that connected us all to God.

Look for Other Books in the Raise the Flag Series
by Nancy Rue

Book One: *Don't Count on Homecoming Queen*
Tobey suspects Coach is up to something sinister at King High, and only the Flagpole Girls can help her figure out what to do!
ISBN 1-57856-032-2

Book Two: *"B" Is for Bad at Getting into Harvard*
Norie's faced with the chance of getting the grades she's worked so hard to attain, at a tremendous cost. Will she cheat or find another way?
ISBN 1-57856-033-0

Book Three: *I Only Binge on Holy Hungers*
Cheyenne only wants to fit in. Shoplifting seems to be the means to an end. It will take her Christian friends to help her find the way out.
ISBN 1-57856-034-9

Book Four: *Do I Have to Paint You a Picture?*
Brianna and the Flagpole Girls learn that keeping the peace is rough business when the rumblings of racial tension escalate into real-life violence.
ISBN 1-57856-035-7

Book Five: *Friends Don't Let Friends Date Jason*
When Marissa finds out that the first boy she's ever fallen for is a user, she learns that a healthy self-esteem is worth more than an inflated ego.
ISBN 1-57856-087-X; *Available in 1999*

Book Six: *Untitled*
Shannon's wonderful Christian family is falling apart because her sister Katelyn has gone wild. Will her parents ever see the "good kid" in Shannon hiding in the shadows?
ISBN 1-57856-088-8; *Available in 1999*

Join millions of other students in praying for your school! See You at the Pole, a global day of student prayer, is the third Wednesday of September each year. For more information, contact:

See You at the Pole
P.O. Box 60134
Fort Worth, TX 76115
24-hour SYATP Hotline: 619/592-9200
Internet: www.syatp.com
e-mail: pray@syatp.com